The
Discontented
Ghost

The Discontented Ghost

by SCOTT CORBETT

A Unicorn Book

E. P. DUTTON   NEW YORK

Library of Congress Cataloging in Publication Data

Corbett, Scott.   The discontented ghost.
(A Unicorn book)
SUMMARY: The resident ghost of an English manor house
vows to rid the property of its new American owner. A
retelling of Oscar Wilde's story "The Canterville Ghost"
from the ghost's point of view.
[1. Ghost stories]   I. Title.
PZ7.C79938Dk   [Fic]   78-18013   ISBN: 0-525-28775-2

Published in the United States by E. P. Dutton, a Division
of Sequoia-Elsevier Publishing Company, Inc., New York
Published simultaneously in Canada by Clarke,
Irwin & Company Limited, Toronto and Vancouver
Editor: Emilie McLeod   Designer: Meri Shardin

Printed in the U.S.A.   First Edition
10 9 8 7 6 5 4 3 2 1

To
Oscar Wilde
and
Sir Arthur Conan Doyle,
with the hope that they
will not haunt me
for my sins

preface

Oscar Wilde's story "The Canterville Ghost," which appeared first in *The Court and Society Review*, February 23 and March 2, 1887, and was published in 1891 in *Lord Arthur Savile's Crime and Other Stories*, is the inspiration of this retelling of the story from the ghost's point of view. Both Sir Simon de Canterville and I will be eternally grateful to Oscar Wilde for his brilliant though somewhat inaccurate account of Sir Simon's adventures, and hope that the reader will consult Mr. Wilde's version, which is readily available.

The
Discontented
Ghost

one

I, SIR SIMON DE CANTERVILLE, have decided it is time to set my record straight. Nearly a hundred years have passed since Oscar Wilde pieced together his account of events, which he called simply *The Canterville Ghost;* and though Oscar was the wittiest of chaps, and a good hand with a pen, when it came to facts he had an Irish inclination.

The time was 1884, the forty-seventh year of the reign of Queen Victoria. The place was a charming corner of Berkshire where for three hundred years I had been the resident ghost of Canterville Chase, my ancestral home, one of the Stately Homes of England so much has been written about. Portions of the seat have been *in situ* from time immemorial. Various noble residents have added to it since the days of Edward the Confessor. My revered ancestor Good Sir Alfred spruced it up quite a bit when he became the first Lord Canterville.

The great house is one of those huge places, half mansion and half castle, with miles of drafty corridors lined with tapestries and paintings and busts and suits of armour—in short, one of those noble piles with great halls and royal bedchambers, with gables and turrets and oriel windows, a battlemented tower or two, wine cellars, dungeons, torture chambers, and all the other good things of life.

One afternoon I was puttering around the house, feeling at loose ends and wishing there was something to do in my line of work. The current Lord Canterville and his family (he was the seventeenth of our illustrious line) had been absent for a long time. I could not understand it, and did not like it. There is little point in being an accomplished ghost if there is no one around to haunt. I was thoroughly discontented.

For want of something better to do I stopped to glare at the portrait of myself a wretched Italian artist named Sbagliorone had painted in 1574. Sbagliorone! In Italian the name means "big mistake," and I am sure he came from a long line of them. I had wanted Hans Holbein the Younger's nephew Ludwig to do the portrait, but he put me off with some trifling excuse, so I was forced to settle for this Sbagliorone scoundrel, who made a botch of it.

He gave me a chin that receded far more than was the actual case, and a pop-eyed look a weasel would have resented. Not to mention thin hair, buck teeth, cup-handle ears, a cucumber nose, and a wart on my left cheek twice as large as the original. I think the Venetian varlet knew from the start I planned to cheat him out of his pay, and thus took mean revenge on me.

So now, here was my poor daub of a portrait stuck away down a side corridor where hardly anyone ever looked at it (the light was generally dismal there, anyway), while the place of honour over the great fireplace in the library was occupied by the seventh earl (known as the Scourge of Southeastern Flanders) merely because he happened to win a battle and had been painted by Van Dyck. For a century or two my portrait was at least given wall space in the great entrance hall because of my spectral celebrity, but the present Lord Canterville had caused it to be banished on aesthetic grounds. While I applauded his good taste, I felt he might have considered my sensibilities, and for several nights after its demotion I picketed his bedchamber, groaning and rattling a sturdy set of chains. He was unmoved.

After brooding on the injustice of it all for a few unhappy moments, I decided to drift on to the library and look for something to read. I felt discouraged at the very thought, however, since the library, though large, was badly in need of fresh material. Thousands of volumes, yes, but in three-hundred years' time, one can turn a lot of pages. I had more than exhausted the collection. Have you ever read Tillworthy's *History of Dulwich* for the third time?

As I trudged dull-eyed and listless along the corridor, I stopped suddenly and my ears (they *are* large, I don't deny it) doubtless perked up somewhat in the manner of a fine hound's. I was startled to realise I could hear the sound of voices coming from somewhere further on in the house.

I had company!

Eager to learn who it was, I hurried forward, but then I paused, remembering that I might be seen. Until I knew who my visitors were and how hauntable they might be I did not want that to happen. Your professional ghost does not come blundering onto the scene at just any old time. He chooses his moment. He sets the stage. He checks the weather. He arranges for evocative atmosphere. Unfirming myself then, thinning myself out to the point of invisibility, I continued on and discovered the voices were coming from the library.

They were two in number. In the cultured tones of one

voice I recognized my lineal descendant, Lord Canterville, but the other was new to me. Whose was that other voice, so nasal and self-assured? It could only be an American's. Later on I learned that the stranger was a statesman whose great wealth had gained him an appointment to Great Britain (an American custom which prevails to this day, I understand). Oscar always referred to Mr. Hiram B. Otis as the American Minister, though if he were actually the ambassador to the Court of St. James, he certainly spent very little of his time tending to his duties during the period in which *I* observed him. But all that came later. On that first occasion I could only surmise that I was listening to some cocksure, purse-proud Yankee who thought he knew it all.

"So this is Canterville Chase! Well, it appears to be pretty much what I've been looking for. Ought to do nicely," he declared. "I'm ready to close the deal."

Lord Canterville cleared his throat in a modulated, well-bred way.

"Really, Mr. Otis? Surely your friends must have urged you not to do so?" he said, and I could sense the millimeter rise of his eyebrows by which he indicated his surprise. "Surely they must have apprised you of Canterville Chase's celebrated—er—encumbrance?"

Meaning yours truly, of course. Being a man of the most punctilious honour he considered himself duty-bound to mention the terrible hazards our American visitor might face were he to rent the ancient house for the summer.

"I don't get you," said Minister Otis. "What do you mean? I suppose you're talking about the plumbing, but I *expect* that to be god-awful. I'll tend to that in my own good time."

"I am not referring to the plumbing, Minister Otis," said

Lord Canterville smoothly, "I am referring to the Canterville Ghost."

"Oh, that."

Now, if you should consult Oscar Wilde's account you will find he had an uncanny ability to reproduce verbatim those of our conversations that were reported to him. Time after time he was word-perfect in setting them down. The following exchanges between Lord Canterville and Minister Otis are good examples.

"We have not cared to live in the place ourselves since my grand-aunt, the dowager duchess of Bolton, was frightened into a fit, from which she never really recovered, by two skeleton hands being placed on her shoulders as she was dressing for dinner. . . ."

So that was it! That was why the family had stayed away for so long! I was shocked and hurt, and also deeply disappointed by my descendant's hypocrisy, since I knew he had always considered the old duchess a bore and a nuisance. Well, it teaches you. One never knows how a kindness will be taken.

Lord Canterville continued:

". . . And I feel bound to tell you, Mr. Otis, that the ghost has been seen by several living members of my family, as well as by the rector of the parish, the Reverend Augustus Dampier, who is a fellow of King's College, Cambridge. After the unfortunate accident to the duchess, none of our younger servants would stay with us, and Lady Canterville often got very little sleep at night, in consequence of the mysterious noises that came from the corridor and the library."

What twaddle! Now Lord Canterville was really embroidering. He knew as well as I did that Lady Canterville's troubles had nothing to do with my efforts. She was a city girl, and all those birds twittering outside her window in the early morning drove her crazy.

Even this exaggeration was wasted on the Minister, however.

"My lord," he said, "I will take the furniture and the ghost at a fair valuation" —meaning that *I* could be thrown in at no extra charge as far as he was concerned! I wished I had not been invisible, so that I could have turned livid with anger.

Peeping round the half-open door, I took a good look at the impudent upstart and saw a short, round, ruddy-faced bald man who reminded me a good deal of another Yankee I had once glimpsed at Canterville Chase some years earlier, another American Minister named John Adams. I wished now I had paid Mr. Adams a good bone-chilling midnight visit.

"I come from a modern country, where we have everything money can buy," Mr. Otis went on in that same rasping, self-assured voice. Americans in those days talked the way Arabs do today. "What with our buying up your best paintings, and carrying off your best actors and actresses to play in New York, and your best sopranos to sing at our opera houses, I reckon if there were such a thing as a ghost in Europe, we'd have it at home in a very short time in one of our public museums, or on the road as a show."

Now he was talking about me as if I were an Egyptian mummy or a trained bear! I can tell you, it was touch and go whether or not I would rush in then and there, shrieking and gibbering, to teach the man a lesson which he—

However, I didn't want to spoil the sale.

Oh, yes—by now I had, of course, realised that this was

no mere summer rental being discussed, but an outright sale. I was surprised to learn that my descendant would consider selling the Chase, but I was not worried. Far from it: I was delighted. Here was a splendid opportunity for a spell of pleasant activity and a chance to add a nice piece of change to the family coffers as well. I even hoped that for once the present Lord Canterville was deserting his ridiculously high principles and pulling a fast one in the good old Canterville tradition that had stood all the rest of us in such good stead—in short, that he had the same scheme in mind that I did. Let the popinjay purchase the place, and then leave the rest to Sir Simon. In no time at all I would throw such a fright into Minister Otis and his family that he would do anything to unload the house, and would be only too glad to sell it back to us at a loss. Though beyond monetary cares myself, I was always eager to see the family stay in the chips.

Meanwhile, Lord Canterville was remaining every inch an Englishman. He was not giving an inch, not one, and he was a tall man. Retaining his suavely British superiority like the nobleman he was, he smilingly replied, "I fear that the ghost exists, though it may have resisted the overtures of your enterprising impresarios. It has been well known for three centuries, since 1584, in fact—exactly three centuries, come to think of it—and always makes its appearance before the death of any member of our family."

"Well, so does the family doctor, for that matter," rejoined the Minister, but again his lordship merely smiled.

"Sir Simon also appears on less formal occasions," he murmured, and shrugged in a genteel way. "However, if you don't mind a ghost in the house, it is all right. Only you must remember I warned you."

Fair enough. If the pigeon still insisted on stepping into

the trap, he could not make any future claims of misrepresentation.

The bargain was sealed. Within a few weeks, at the close of the London season, Mr. Hiram B. Otis and his family, whoever they might consist of, would be taking up residence at Canterville Chase. With demoniac though silent glee, I rubbed my invisible hands together.

"But not for long, you won't, Minister Yankee Doodle!" I promised him in an inaudible whisper, "not for long!"

two

THE NEXT FEW WEEKS were busy ones as I prepared for our visitors.

All the gowns, shrouds, habits, and other trappings of my extensive repertoire of roles had to be taken out and given a good airing beneath the yew trees and weeping willows that cast their melancholy shade over the family burial ground. I would hang them out at night and bring them back in the morning, smelling deliciously of mould and mildew and the vapours of the tomb. And as I bustled about, my mind grappled with the pleasant task of selection. Which one from among my many celebrated performances should be called upon to rid Canterville Chase of this infestation of Americans? Red Ruben, or the Strangled Babe, for example, or Gaunt Gibeon, the Bloodsucker of Bexley Moor? There were so many stellar roles to choose from, each more frightful than the last, each with its happy memories of past triumphs.

In the circumstances I had become rabidly anti-American. My attitude toward Minister Otis was ferocious. I longed to show him no mercy, I longed to reduce him to a quivering jelly; only my sense of duty to Queen and Country prevented me from planning dangerous excesses. I reminded myself that Minister Otis was an American of considerable prominence and political importance. It would be one thing to frighten the Otises sufficiently to send them fleeing, but quite another to cause permanent mental disorder or even a death or two in the family. Anything on that scale could have serious diplomatic repercussions. It might even lead to war, and I told myself that another war with the Colonies would be an unmitigated disaster, since if we won we would have to take them back. In short, a fine touch was called for, just so much and no more, always keeping in mind that my mission was merely to rid Canterville Chase, not the world, of the Otis blight.

Early in June came the day when the interlopers were to put in an appearance. Not a detail escaped me. I knew they were to arrive by an afternoon train at Ascot, the nearest railway station, seven miles distant. Two sturdy crofters from the nearby village of Canterville Coomb were to meet the train with a waggonette to bring them and their luggage to their new residence. The waggonette was an open four-wheeled carriage with side seats facing each other and a seat or two crosswise in front, sometimes covered but in this case not. By now I had also learned that the family consisted of the Minister's wife, a handsome matron of serenely commanding presence, and four children. The eldest was Washington, a lad of twenty, followed by Miss Virginia, a young lady of fifteen, followed by John and Ronald, twins of ten.

This was the group, then, that was approaching its doom on a lovely June evening when, as Oscar pointed out, "the air was delicate with the scent of the pinewoods. Now and then they heard a wood pigeon brooding over its own sweet voice, or saw, deep in the rustling fern, the burnished breast of the pheasant. Little squirrels peeped at them from the beech-trees as they went by, and the rabbits scudded away through the brushwood and over the mossy knolls, with their white tails in the air."

All very well, that, but hardly the proper atmosphere in which to introduce these rash intruders to their new surroundings. A change to something more suitably gloomy and sinister was called for, and this requirement was taken care of by a confederate of mine, of whom more later.

With entire appropriateness the change occurred as the waggonette swung into the long private drive that ran through dark woods to the front of the great house. Clouds gathered overhead with curious abruptness. The atmosphere, suddenly still, trembled with portent. Black and satanic, a great flight of rooks passed silently overhead. Before the newcomers reached the house, a spattering of raindrops, large and cold, caused the ladies to cry out in dismay and wish for umbrellas to protect their frocks—but of course the Minister had not thought to bring any. Americans never do. On the driver's seat of the waggonette Alf Muggins and Jeremy Gouge exchanged nervous glances and licked dry lips while sweat began to crisscross down deep channels in the rough hide of their red necks. Of course their lips were chronically dry any time they found themselves more than ten paces from a public house, but this was an accentuated dryness. By the time the vehicle cleared the woods and rolled up before the broad front steps of the noble edifice, their beefy faces were as long as two square Saxon faces could possibly be.

Thanks to Lady Canterville, a reception committee of one awaited the Otises. This was Mrs. Umney, the housekeeper, whom Lady Canterville had urged Mrs. Otis to retain in her former position. Standing on the steps to receive them, neatly dressed in black silk, with a white cap and apron, the old woman made them each a low curtsey as they alighted, making six low curtseys in all—no, five; she let the twins split a curtsey; but at any rate enough low curtseys to put her old bones to a severe test. Puffing slightly from the exertion, she then said in a quaint, old-fashioned manner, "I bid you welcome to Canterville Chase."

The quaint welcome taken care of, she turned her attention to the help.

"Alf and Jemmy, you'll bring that luggage into the great hall," she ordered, "and there we'll see about what's to go upstairs to which chambers."

By now the men's lips were not merely dry, they were cracked. Their tongues rasped across them like files as their pinched glances darted together and apart again.

"Beggin' yer pardon, us'll set the traps out on the top o' yon steps," rumbled Alf, "but us ain't nuther of us settin' foot inside. Us wants naught to do with 'im!"

Minister Otis swung around, an amazed little turkey-cock of a man.

"Im?" he cried. "Who's Im?"

"'Im," repeated Alf, pawing the ground with his clod-hopper feet. He was, of course, referring to the very 'im who was at that moment unobtrusively observing the scene from the oriel window above. "The 'ouse is 'aunted, that it is!"

The Minister laughed sharply.

"Oh, come now! Surely you don't believe such foolishness!"

"Us knows what us knows," put in Jemmy, speaking as darkly as had Alf, if not a shade darker.

"Ay, Jemmy, that we do," agreed Alf and, liking the roll of the phrase, repeated it several times.

The oxlike breadth of their low foreheads told the Minister he would get nowhere with arguments and recriminations, so he took a sharper tack.

"Not even for an extra shilling apiece, lads?" he asked, jingling his pockets suggestively, and added a blatant appeal. "Is this the spirit that has made British soldiery famous the world around?"

Thin red lines threaded across the hollow square of their brows, and thick tongues once again reminded them how parched they were.

"Well, puttin' it that way, sir," rumbled Alf, glancing again at Jemmy for support, "mayhaps we could set 'em just inside the door."

"Hm. Well, it appears as if it may rain again, so I suppose that will have to do," said Minister Otis, producing the shillings. "Get on with it."

Preceded by Mrs. Umney, the Otises trooped inside. Seizing pieces of luggage, Alf and Jemmy rushed back and forth with feverish haste. I waited till they had started up the steps with their final load, then stepped into full view at the oriel window and tapped on a pane. They glanced up.

"Bullabullabullabullabullabullabulla!"

I gave them a thorough gibbering, tongue flapping like flannel, eyeballs out on sticks. Boxes and parcels dropped from hands gone numb, eyeballs imitated my own.

"Ai! It's 'im!"

In two bounds they were in the carriage and whipping up their surprised team, and within seconds they disappeared round a bend in the drive on two wheels.

"Here! Come back!" Young Washington Otis had rushed out of the house. He stared after them, shook his head, and began gathering up some of the dropped parcels. Thinning myself out, I hurried downstairs, not wanting to miss the first glimmerings of uneasiness the Otises were about to experience.

Mrs. Umney had laid out a nice tea for them in the library. Oscar, who never actually saw the house, described the library as a "long, low room," which is wrong, unless you call a room low that contains a twelve-foot ladder for use in reaching the topmost bookshelves. He was right, however, about the panelling, which was dark oak, and about the large stained-glass window at the far end of the room. The furnishings avoided the worst excesses of the late Victorian era, without emphasizing any particular period of the past. Under the stained-glass window a portrait of Good Sir Alfred glared sideways with jealous eyes at the Van Dyck over the mantelpiece. I perched invisibly on a bookcase beneath Sir Alfred and was ready to enjoy myself.

The family had taken off their wraps, and Mrs. Otis was telling Mrs. Umney how nice the tea service looked, and Minister Otis was muttering something about wondering if a feller could get a cup of coffee around here, and the twins were snitching cucumber sandwiches from a carefully arranged tray, and Miss Virginia was ordering them to stop it, when Washington returned to the library with a puzzled expression on his face.

"Those two bumpkins suddenly dropped everything and lit out as if the devil were after them," he reported.

"What?" cried the Minister. "Why?"

"Something seemed to throw a scare into them. They looked up at the house, at that big window that sticks out, and they all but jumped out of their skins. They said something about Im again, and then they lit out."

A plate shattered on the floor.

"The Curse of the Cantervilles," groaned Mrs. Umney,

clutching the back of a chair for support. "I am sorry, madam. I did not expect it to come so soon." And she stooped to gather up the fragments of the plate.

But Mrs. Otis was not listening. Instead she was shaking her head in a disapproving way and sighing, "Oh, dear, what a shame. Now I suppose they'll simply drink up that money you gave them, Hiram."

I silently agreed, and would have been willing to bet that the Minister's two shillings would be in the till at the Bull and Buskin in Canterville Coomb within five minutes. I would have lost, however, for as it happened Alf Muggins missed the sharp turn just before the highroad and took a wheel off the carriage. They had to run the rest of the way, and were two minutes late.

"I knew I shouldn't have paid the rascals till they finished every lick of the work," grumbled the Minister, jingling his pockets irritably.

"Well, never mind, I'm sure we can manage," said Mrs. Otis. "Come have your tea, Washington."

"I wonder if that woman can make a decent cup of coffee," the Minister speculated as Mrs. Umney tottered out of the room with the broken plate.

"Mmmm, these cucumber sandwiches are delicious!" said Miss Virginia. I must confess that Oscar did her no more than simple justice when he described her as "lithe and lovely as a fawn, and with a fine freedom in her blue eyes." She concentrated those finely free blue eyes severely on the twins. "Mama, make them stop gobbling all the sandwiches."

"Why? I'm hungry!" said Johnny.

"And *I'm* hungry!" said Ronny.

"Mind your sister, you greedy little pigs!" snarled Washington, grabbing three or four sandwiches. He was a tall, gangly youth with large hands and feet—in fact, he was like a puppy not quite grown into its paws.

"Now, children, that will do," said Mrs. Otis. "Drink your milk, boys, and stop trying to swallow everything whole."

She glanced round her with a planning eye.

"This room is quite nice, or at any rate it will be as soon as we change these sofas around and move several of the tables. And that armchair, surely it should be . . . Hiram, would you just pick it up and—"

But instead the Minister sat down firmly in the chair, as though to anchor it to the spot.

"Lucretia, I am *not* going to start moving furniture around just yet! I can't even have a cup of coffee, but at least let me finish swilling this vile tea—"

His wife gave him an indulgent little smile.

"Oh, very well, Hiram, I suppose I'll have to spoil you just this once."

At that moment, as Mrs. Umney returned to the room, Mrs. Otis's housewifely eye was attracted to a very noticeable dull red stain on the floor in front of the fireplace. She leaned forward for a better look, and pointed to it.

"Dear me. Mrs. Umney, I am afraid something has been spilt there."

The old housekeeper's step faltered. She seemed to repress a shudder as she responded in a low voice.

"Yes, madam. Blood has been spilt on that spot."

"Blood?" Mrs. Otis gave her a look much as to say that British housekeeping standards, never high in her estimation, had gone down another notch. "How horrid! I don't at all care for bloodstains in a sitting room. It must be removed at once."

The old woman's smile did not quite conceal her disdain

for this ignorant request as she answered in the same low, mysterious voice.

"It is the blood of Lady Eleanore de Canterville, who was murdered on that very spot by her husband, Sir Simon de Canterville, in 1575. Sir Simon survived her nine years, and disappeared suddenly under very mysterious circumstances. His body has never been discovered, but his guilty spirit still haunts the Chase. The bloodstain has been much admired by tourists and others, and cannot be removed."

Now, I think you will agree that such a revelation as that should have gotten terror off to a good rousing start. At the very least Mrs. Otis should have swooned, and Miss Virginia gone off into hysterics. It was Washington Otis, however, who was first to react. He sprang up and quickly left the room.

"Why, what is the matter with Washington?" wondered his mother, and I longed to reply, "He is a sensitive boy, madam, and he is fleeing from . . . he knows not what." But before anyone could answer the worried mother, her son was back, and clutched in his hand was a fat, shiny stick of some repulsive-looking black substance, which he waved confidently aloft.

"This is all nonsense!" he cried. "Pinkerton's Champion Stain Remover and Paragon Detergent will clean it up in no time."

And before the terrified housekeeper could interfere, the young vandal was down on his hands and knees scouring the floor with the evil stuff.

"No, no!" cried Mrs. Umney, trying to get at him but failing because the twins were in the way. "That stain cannot be—"

But by then there was not a trace of it left to be seen. Washington held up his presumptuous weapon.

"I knew Pinkerton would do it!" he exclaimed triumphantly, as he looked around at his admiring family. But no sooner had he finished his odious gloat than a terrible flash of lightning sent blood-red fire through the great stained-glass window, a fearful peal of thunder made them all start to their feet, and Mrs. Umney fainted.

For an instant they all stood in a dramatic tableau, staring down at the insensible woman. It was Mrs. Otis who finally spoke.

"Oh, dear," said she. "Washington, run out into the hall and bring in my Red Cross first aid kit, will you, please?"

Washington hastened to do her bidding. He returned carrying a square wooden box with a red cross prominently displayed on its top. She opened it, removed one or two trays, and found the small bottle she wanted. Uncorking it, she handed it to the miscreant.

"Hold this under the poor woman's nose, dear."

Stooping, Washington did so, whereupon Mrs. Umney shot to her feet with a shriek.

"Lord a' mercy, what was that?" she cried, clutching her temples. "It fair took the top of my head off!"

"Armbruster's Supreme Smelling Salts," replied Mrs. Otis in a voice disciplined to remain steady. "It never fails. Virginia, will you please help Mrs. Umney to her room and tuck her into bed? I am afraid Washington has given her something of a shock."

"Two," muttered Mrs. Umney as she allowed herself to be helped toward the door. But then in the doorway she pulled herself together and turned around with her eyes flashing wildly and an arm raised in solemn warning.

"Take care, take care!" she croaked. "I have seen things with my own eyes that would make any Christian's hair stand on end, and many and many a night I have not closed my eyes in sleep for the awful things that are done here!"

"That reminds me," said Minister Otis, "is there a Baptist church anywhere in the neighbourhood?"

"Baptist!" Mrs. Umney rolled her eyes upward, turned, and was gone. It was all Miss Virginia could do to keep up with her.

As soon as Mrs. Umney was out of sight and earshot, Mrs. Otis's expression underwent a change from that of calm matron to stern mother.

"All right, now," she said, turning to the twins, "which one of you has been meddling with my smelling salts?"

Both boys responded instantly, and with the same word— "Him."

"I see. In other words, both of you," said their mother, trapping them neatly. "My smelling salts are powerful, but not *that* powerful. Hiram?"

Sighing, the Minister had already disappeared into the hallway. He returned with a well-worn birch rod, which he obviously found necessary to carry with him everywhere. The entire history of the twins' misdeeds was doubtless imprinted on its worn surface. Automatically, as though from force of habit, the boys assumed the position, and the Minister laid six of the best alternately on their round bottoms. When he had finished the operation, which the little devils underwent without flinching, Mrs. Otis gave them a lecture on the perils of fiddling with first aid kits and told them they were never, never to touch hers again.

They listened solemnly till she had finished, and then Ronny broke into an irrepressible grin.

"Didn't she just jump, though!" he said.

"Didn't she, though!" agreed Johnny.

And do you know, in a moment they had the whole of

that heartless family—save Miss Virginia, who had not yet returned—laughing in spite of themselves.

The battle lines were drawn, and all mercy went out of me. I decided then and there that their ordeal at Canterville Chase would be no ordinary one. If this meant war, let it come!

three

Now that the matter of Lady Eleanore has come up, and my own sudden disappearance "under very mysterious circumstances," I suppose this is as good a time as any to make a clean breast of the actual facts, even though some of them fill me with shame. I feel I must force myself to disclose them, since here is one of the places where Oscar really shot wide of the mark. Of course, one cannot blame him. He only knew what had been reported.

He did quote me accurately, however, as to a statement I once had occasion to make about Lady Eleanore:

"My wife was very plain, never had my ruffs properly starched, and knew nothing about cookery. Why, there was a buck I had shot in Hogley Woods, a magnificent pricket, and do you know how she had it sent up to table?"

She was then eight-and-twenty, and I a year older. We had been married for eight years. Everything in my statement was justified except for a slight exaggeration as to her plainness, which I threw in for effect at the time. She was plain, yes, but not *very* plain. By your standards today, what with her long straight sleek black hair, her high cheekbones, and her unusual greenish-grey eyes, she might even be judged not bad-looking at all, especially considering her really superb figure. But all the rest of my statement toed the mark.

Speaking of that pricket, as far as her demise was concerned it was that very pricket that brought about the happy event and provided me with the best nine years of my life.

Having bagged the creature, I invited to dinner a large group of friends and enemies—in those days it was hard to tell which were which, as you must know if you have read your Shakespeare. I confidently expected that evening to be one of the great social triumphs of my life. I looked forward to observing with insolent eyes the ill-concealed envy of Sir Mordred Montague, with whom I had long feuded over faggot-gathering rights to a forest in which our property lines met, and the jealous spleen of Lord Braceley of Braceley Hall, who disputed order of precedence with me every time we entered mutual friends' dining halls. Great would be their mortification and dark their thoughts when they saw the Pricket Supreme I planned to set before them that night.

You can scarcely conceive, then, of my confusion and embarrassment when I saw what Lady Eleanore had caused to be done with the main course. My triumph was ashes in my mouth, and compared to the rest of the food, the ashes tasted good. The guests coped by simply getting even drunker than usual. I thought they would never leave.

When at long last the final guest had been carried out and sent on his way, I flew into a passion and sent a servant with kicks and blows to summon Lady Eleanore to the library. Standing in front of the fireplace, feet planted well apart, hands clenched behind my back, I glanced up at the portrait of Good Sir Alfred, who still had the place of honour in those days, and drew grim resolve from his fiery scowl.

When Lady Eleanore appeared, her habitual taunting and supercilious smile was on her face. That was what our marriage had come to by then—smiles of that description whenever we were tête-à-tête. And as usual she was knitting away on something sixty to the minute. Oh, how I hated the click of those long, slim, steel knitting needles—Number 2s, they were, I have since learned. In recent years I have taken up a bit of knitting now and then myself and find it very relaxing; but in those days, because of her, I detested every form of such handiwork. For one thing, she never found time to knit a nice pair of mittens for *me*, or anything like that—oh, no, it was always scarves for the servants or the village needy!

She made me a deep, mocking curtsey and said, "Well, my lord, what is it now?"

"Thou knowest full well what it is!" I retorted hotly. "I was never so humiliated! That buck—"

"I loved that buck," she murmured. "He had thy teeth."

"Quip me no quips!" I roared. "The buck was overcooked—King Henry himself couldn't have eaten it—but that wasn't the worst of it! What ever possessed thee to have it sent up to table *whole*, with an apple in its mouth?"

She batted her eyelids in simulated innocence.

"Is that not the standard recipe, my lord?"

"No, no, thou fool, 'tis boars that have apples in their mouths!"

She turned, took an apple from a bowl, and handed it to me.

"Prithee put one in thy mouth so that I may see how a bore looketh."

I hurled the apple into the fireplace.

"Not that kind of bore, saucepot—B-O-A-R, with bristles!"

"Thou hast bristles," she pointed out, "right on the end of thy wart."

There was no abiding the virago. From a collection of arms arranged on the mantelpiece I seized a Florentine stiletto, complete with bejewelled handle and scabbard, which I had once picked up in a little shop on the Ponte Vecchio.

"Another jest like that," I cried, "an' 't will be thy last!"

Her laughter trilled out, but then the blackness of my brow proved enough to alarm even her, and she whirled around to hurry away.

As she did so her foot caught in a ragged rent in the great Hamadan carpet an ancestor on my grandmother's side had brought back from the Crusades.

If I had told her once I had told her a hundred times to have Tom the Weaver come in and fix that rip.

She tumbled forward, fell heavily on her face, uttered a piercing cry, and rolled slowly onto her back.

A pierced cry, I should have said. One of her Number 2 knitting needles was sticking straight up from her shapely bosom.

Her eyes were opened in a fixed stare of horror that quickly turned glassy. I knelt beside her and pressed my head against her breast, listening for heartbeats. All I accomplished, however, was to get a good deal of blood on my ear. She was dead.

I was in a panic. You can understand my position. The servants had surely heard our quarrel, they were always hanging around, listening behind doors. What would they think? What would be left of the family honour, were even one of them to blunder in and observe what had happened before I had a chance to stop him? If ever it got around that my clumsy clod of a wife had died by falling on her own knitting needle, we Cantervilles would never live it down! We would be the laughingstock of every shire. Noble-women simply did not die in such lower-class ways. Look at Shakespeare's plays. Look at Webster's. With a woman of breeding it had to be high tragedy, a melodramatic suicide or a classy murder, preferably at the hands of someone of equally impeccable social standing. But instead, she had left me with this scandal on my hands. It was just like her. What was I to do? How—

The stiletto!

Suddenly I was aware that the Florentine stiletto was still in my hand. I examined its exquisitely worked handle, its dazzling scabbard. Yes, it was worthy. I would have paid at least twenty ducats for it, if I had paid for it. I drew the thin blade from its scabbard and found it to be—

Perfect!

A Number 2-size stiletto if ever I had seen one!

Carefully I drew the knitting needle from Lady Elea-nore's breast and replaced it with the stiletto. A slightly tight fit, perhaps, but a few smart taps drove it home. I had wiped the needle clean and hidden it in my doublet and was tidy-ing up my ear by the time the first servant summoned up enough courage to enter the room and quaver, "B-be they aught amiss, m'lord?"

Well, there was a great to-do about the matter, of course, but I went scot-free. I had known I would. All I had to do was call as witnesses several of the noblemen who had been among the guests that evening when the pricket was sent up to table. In fact, the local magistrate, Sir Gawain Glut-worthy, had been among the guests and had suffered from indigestion all night long after forcing down his helpings of the buck. A verdict of justifiable uxoricide was speedily returned, and I went home.

From that moment forward my life was utterly changed. When a man is thought to have murdered his wife it gives him a certain panache he would not otherwise have. I became a popular figure. I was asked to dinner far oftener than ever before—in truth, I dined out on the story for at least a year. And naturally, as time went on, I improved the story, until I almost grew to believe it myself. Safe from any threat of disclosure of my true shame, I went on living a lie with ruthless pleasure and with scarcely a twinge of conscience.

For one thing, I never again appeared in company anywhere without the famous stiletto at my side. Needless to say, everyone wanted to see it. You should have heard the ladies ooh and aah over it!

Speaking of the ladies, my new lustre proved invaluable to me in that department. Where once they had avoided my eyes with a yawn or even a slight shudder, they still shuddered, but in a different way. Deliciously, you might say. Yes, indeed, many a sparkling glance was cast Sir Simon-ward now. A dangerous lover has a great appeal to women. Dalliance was mine, and I made the most of it. And I grew more and more conceited.

Inevitably, of course, because of my great name, there were those dowagers with marriageable daughters who began to bait their traps for me. One evening, when I had laid on a splendid dinner at Canterville Chase to pay off some of my social obligations, a dinner at which my new French chef had given us a *pricket aux champignons bordelais* that melted in our mouths, a dowager duchess much like that dreadful old dowager duchess of Bolton—an ancestress of hers, in fact—took it upon herself to remark archly,

"How now, Sir Simon, is not nine years a long while to stay without a helpmeet? And when shall we have a new Lady Canterville?"

Now, dalliance was one thing, but marriage, as I had learned to my sorrow, was quite another. I was now thirty-eight years of age, with a sixteen-year-old son and a fourteen-year-old daughter, so the succession was provided for, and I felt no pressing need for more daughters to have to worry about marrying off. I should have passed off the beldame's impertinence with a laugh, but instead I let pride in my borrowed plumes get away from me—pride in my undeserved fame as a wife-murderer, that is to say.

Giving my head an insouciant waggle, and allowing an enigmatic smile to twitch at the corners of my mouth, I drew out the famous stiletto and delicately touched the tip of it with my finger.

"Ah, yes," I murmured, playing my part shamelessly, "who shall be next?"

At that instant a terrible flash of lightning and clap of thunder filled and shook the room, and a great deep voice that only I could hear said:

"All right, lad, you've had it!"

Voices from on high are timeless. They speak any idiom, past, present, or future, that suits them. The expression, which would only become current four centuries later, was unfamiliar, but its meaning was perfectly clear. Something cataclysmic had happened to me. I felt all fizzy from head to toe, as though I were filled with that carbonated swill Americans guzzle so much of. One instant I had this fizzy feeling, and the next instant I was no longer on the premises, but floating around somewhere in space.

Meanwhile, back at the Chase, a distinguished gathering

of lords and ladies, as well as varlets and serving wenches, were picking themselves up off the floor and trying to decide what had happened. The only thing they could agree on was that their genial host, Sir Simon, was gone. Vanished. Disappeared suddenly.

Under very mysterious circumstances.

four

I MUST SAY I was a bit confused myself. As for that voice from on high, however, I soon decided it had not come from as high as I had assumed. Not nearly so high. I was sure I had the wrong powers in mind entirely. Because who do you suppose was the first being I saw after I had floated around for a while in a greyish sort of vapour?

None other than my blasted wife, Lady Eleanore!

When the greyish vapour cleared away, there we were, face to face, and hers was severe.

"Simon, you are the limit!" she scolded. "I didn't mind your ridiculous airs at first, in fact I got a good laugh out of them, but you finally went too far! For some time I've known you would, so I pulled a few strings and got permission to end your silly posturing and have you assigned to some useful work. For one thing, if you had gone on much longer you probably *would* have married again and spoiled the succession."

The easy authority of her speech astonished and alarmed me. How came it she was in a position to pull strings? What was she doing here—wherever "here" was—and what nasty little trick did she have up her long black sleeve? What did she mean by that reference to having me assigned to "useful work"? Among those who did useful work were galley slaves, unskilled labour recruited for salt mines, and Turkish harem attendants carefully divested of all possible conflicts of interest. I could picture my dear wife gleefully arranging my reincarnation in the form of any one of these unfortunates. Though I confess to quaking inwardly, I did my best to keep up a bold front as I put a sharp question to her.

"Madam, how is it you have so much say in these matters?"

She smiled complacently.

"That knitting needle had scarce pierced my heart before They were offering me a very good position."

"They?"

"Avast with too much curiosity!" she warned with a scowl, whilst an ominous rumble seemed to come from somewhere around us, too close for comfort. "Just be satisfied with They."

I was convinced.

"All right, then, They," I said hastily. "But . . . what was this position They offered you?"

She drew herself up proudly.

"Witchhood!"

"Witchhood?" Now an icy fear really gripped my heart, and yet I was cursed if I would grovel before that woman, come what may. "Well, They certainly knew promising material when They saw it," I said bitterly. "They'd probably been scouting you for years."

"Have a care with thy insolent tongue else I treat thee to a sup of something I brewed but yestereve in a bubbling cauldron," she retorted. "If thou thinkest that pricket was bad . . ."

I shrugged wearily.

"Spare me further vaunting. 'Tis plain you have the upper hand. What is this new misery you have in store for me?"

She surprised me with a look of surprise.

"Misery? Who said anything about misery?"

"What else would you wish on me?"

She sighed, and shook her head.

"Now, listen, Simon, we're going to see each other from time to time for . . . well, for a long time, so there's no point in our eternally talking to each other like an ordinary married couple. I had enough of that when we were together."

"*You* had enough?" I groaned. "Are you forgetting that the last words I heard from you were enough to make me seize that foul Florentine pigsticker?"

"No, I'm not forgetting that. But what I want you to understand, Simon, is that I bear no grudge against you. You didn't kill me, and furthermore I quite appreciated the way you shielded our good name from the shame of my having died in such an uncouth way."

"Did you, by George!" I was pleasantly surprised. "I'm glad to hear that. Can you imagine what it would have been like if—"

"We would never have lived it down."

"Never!"

"Very well, then. So you can stop quaking in your boots—"

"I am not quaking in my boots!" I lied angrily, but she merely chuckled in an irritating way.

"Call it what you will, but hark to what I have to say. Now, what do you suppose your assignment is to be?"

"I haven't the ghost of an idea."

She laughed.

33

"That's very well put, Simon."

"I'm sorry, I don't take your meaning."

"You're going to be the Ghost of Canterville Chase."

"The—what? The—the Ghost of—"

"I believe that is what I said."

"Elly! Are you sure?"

"Yes!"

"You mean, I'm going to become a ghost?"

"You *are* a ghost."

"Already?"

"Already."

I was shaken. A ghost! It was a concept that took some getting used to. Not exactly relaxing news at all. But then, as I thought it over I swiftly came to the conclusion I could have done worse. For instance, it beat dying.

Still, I felt called upon to grouse a little.

"I suppose this is your idea of a joke!"

"What do you mean? I thought you'd be pleased!" She stamped her foot and flew into a rage. "Simon, thou ninny, thou witling, knowest thee not a good thing when thou seest it? What frightest thou, poltroon?"

I held up my hands. "Now, stay thy yammering and let me think."

Hastily I returned to a consideration of the positive aspects of my situation. If I had to be a ghost, I would certainly prefer to be one in familiar surroundings. The chance to haunt my own house, where I could keep an eye on the family, and keep them on their toes as well . . . yes, I could do worse.

I nodded crisply.

"Very well. Count me in."

"That's better."

"Maybe so—but what did you mean when you said we'd

be seeing each other from time to time? How frequently—"

"Not often, I'll warrant ye, if I have the say of it!"

"Good. I can't say the sight of you delights me any more now than it did nine years ago."

"Nor you me!"

"Then I'm surprised you bothered."

"I told you why I did it."

"Oh, yes, of course. The succession. Well, you needn't have worried, our son Alfred would have remained next in line no matter how many more children I sired. You never *could* get things like that straight."

"How were the children when you left?"

"Both were well. Gertrude had the sniffles, but then she usually does. Alfred had a chambermaid, but that's to be expected."

"We should never have named him after the first earl. He's going to take it as a challenge."

"Well, the wench is a saucy piece, so I don't blame him."

My thoughts having turned to physical charms, I ran my eye appraisingly up and down Lady Eleanore and did her justice.

"Well, Elly, I must say you've kept your figure."

"Thank you, my lord. I can't say as much for you, though—I don't fancy that little pot you've developed. Sbagliorone would have loved to add that to your account."

I glanced down and saw to my horror that it was still with me.

"Don't tell me I'll still have it now that I'm a ghost!"

"You will unless you start doing some exercises. All that dining out did it, I suppose—"

"Exercises? You mean, those loathsome calisthenic things? But that's unfair! How can I do exercises when I'm practically transparent?"

35

"Don't worry, once you've learned how to firm up you'll have plenty of opportunities."

"What do you mean, firm up?"

"You'll find out, all in good time. Which reminds me, we'd better get down to business, because I can't stay here much longer talking to you. So let me outline your responsibilities."

She now informed me that, as Oscar correctly set it down, it would be "my solemn duty to appear in the corridor once a week, and to gibber from the large oriel window on the first and third Wednesday of every month." Apart from this light schedule I was free to improvise any extra appearances and special events I cared to.

"Fair enough," I said. "When do I start?"

Lady Eleanore gave me a haughty look.

"Listen to him! What do you know about haunting? There's more to it than you think. I can assure you our English ghosts learn their trade just as rigorously as do our English butlers. Before you take up your duties at Canterville Chase you will be put through a good training school, and you will find it pays."

She was right. I learned a great deal at Apparition Academy, and came out prepared to make my old school proud of me. And for three centuries I did just that. I became a celebrated ghost. All went well, except for occasional visits from Lady Eleanore, and even those seemed easier to bear as time went on. Yes, all went well—until those impossible Americans thrust themselves on the scene. We must now return to *them*.

After the deplorable imbroglio in the library I hurried back to my room in the ancient left wing of the house, a long-forgotten room once known as the Tapestry Chamber, and sat down to consider what was to be done. I had scarcely dropped into an ancient armchair when there came a tap at the door. I was not startled. The secret door into the room was so cunningly fitted into the wall of the gloomy passageway leading to the back stairs that no one could have guessed at its existence.

"Come!" I called softly, for my visitor could be only one person.

She entered.

"Ah, Mrs. Umney!"

"I'm in a hurry, Simon, so I didn't bother to change," she said, and sank into my second-best chair with a sigh.

My grin was sardonic.

"That's all right, Elly," I said, for of course it was she. The real Mrs. Umney, whose identity she had assumed, had suffered a mysterious attack of amnesia during the family's absence and was now, thanks to a mysterious anonymous legacy, living contentedly at a seaside resort under the name of Mrs. Effingham.

"Feeling better?" I asked.

"I never felt bad," she snapped, "but I had to do something to impress them, so I fainted."

My snicker was heartless.

"Well, you certainly didn't impress them much. Armbruster's Supreme Smelling Salts brought you around quickly enough!"

"A pox on it! What foul thing will those Yankee quacks concoct next? It was worse than anything I could conjure up out of my own cauldron!"

I cleared up her confusion with a lively description of the events that followed her tottering departure.

"Why, that brace of misbegotten brats!—Simon, you must teach those twins a lesson!"

"Never you fear, I intend to."

"See that you do. But first things first. As soon as I could get rid of the girl I flew over here to see you, because you must do something about that bloodstain, and soon!"

Now it was my turn to wax wroth.

"Vandalism! Vandalism, that's what it was!"

"I quite agree, but name-calling won't get us anywhere now. It's no use crying over spilt blood that's gone."

"Don't worry, I'll think of something. I'd already begun working on the problem when you interrupted me," I lied.

Lady Eleanore gave me a sharp glance.

"All right, Sherlock, I'm glad to hear it—but make it good. I just wanted to remind you," she said, and leapt up nervously. "I must go back now. I must stage a quick recovery, because I'll have to prepare some sort of dinner for them."

I sat up in astonishment.

"What? *You're* going to cook for them?"

"Well, who else? Except for two parlourmaids who are coming in the morning, none of the staff has been engaged as yet, so—"

I rocked in my chair slapping my knee.

"Zounds, I had forgot we had such a secret weapon in our arsenal! Wait till they taste your cooking!"

"Oh, shut up!" snapped Lady Eleanore from the door.

"Try your charred lamb shanks on them, or your—"

But the door had already closed behind her, and none too gently.

Chuckling, I sat back in my chair again, and my chuckles gradually died away as my mind returned to the difficulties that faced me. Something had to be done, yes, but what, and how? Thoughts of the twins, the Minister, Mrs. Otis,

Washington, and Miss Virginia passed through my mind, then thoughts of all the luggage and hatboxes and chests and other paraphernalia that had been slipped hastily inside the door by Alf and Jemmy. Yes, indeed, something had to be done.

five

THE FIRST MEMBER of the family to enter the library after breakfast the next morning was the Minister himself. He walked in with his nose buried in *The Times*, already growling over what Americans call an editorial and we call a leader. He was so absorbed in his reading that he walked without looking to the place where he had taken tea the day before and slowly sat down, groping vaguely behind him with one hand for the arm of the chair. He groped in vain. His well-padded bottom hit the carpet with a thump, his newspaper went flying, and his legs scissored into the air.

"What the blazes—!" He sat up and glared around the room. "By heavens, she's already been in here moving the furniture! Lucretia!"

His angry bellow brought no immediate results. I will say one thing for Mrs. Otis, she never lost her dignity nor her aplomb. In this case, as in most cases, she came at her own stately pace. Fuming, the Minister scrambled to his feet and waited. When she appeared he waved an accusing finger at her like a pistol barrel.

"Lucretia, you've been moving the furniture in here!"

She smiled, as though pleased he had noticed. "Yes. The children helped me. Isn't it infinitely better now?"

"*Better?* I like to killed myself sitting down where a chair was supposed to be!"

"Not again? Hiram, will you never learn to look around at a chair and make sure it's there before you sit in it?"

"No, I'm an incurable optimist!"

Washington strolled in with a grin on his face any father would have found irritating.

"What, has Pa done it again?"

"We don't need any smart-aleck comments from you, Wash," snapped the Minister, and he stooped to gather up his newspaper. As he did so his gaze was arrested by an unexpected sight. He paused in mid-stoop for a stare, moved closer, and stared again.

Instead of recoiling with the cry of horror one might have expected, he straightened up with a grimly satisfied expression on his face. He turned and shot a sarcastic look at his son.

"Pinkerton's Champion Stain Remover and Paragon Detergent, eh? And to think I let you talk me into buying a block of stock in that tinhorn Myers and Podmore outfit!"

Wash—what a nickname!—Wash flushed.

"What are you talking about, Pa?"

His father pointed at the floor.

"If you think that miracle worker of yours took care of the bloodstain, you've got another think coming. It's back."

At last the stain called forth a look of horror from someone. But then it was succeeded on Wash's face by an expression of stubborn faith.

"I don't think it can be the fault of the Paragon Detergent," he said. "I've tried it with everything, and it never fails. So it must be the ghost."

His sister, Virginia, who had followed him into the room, looked down at the stain thoughtfully.

"Yes," she murmured, "it must be the ghost."

Perched invisibly in my customary place on the bookcase under the stained-glass window and Good Sir Alfred's portrait, I was heartened by the votes I was picking up. Little Miss Virginia, now, it was rather dear of her to come through so unhesitatingly, throwing her support to me on the first ballot.

At that point the twins scampered in and took a look.

"Coo!" said Ronny.

"Ronny!" said Mrs. Otis. "Wherever did you pick up that common expression?"

"From Johnny."

"No, you didn't!" said Johnny, "I got it from you!" And with that they were rolling on the carpet in fierce fraternal battle.

"Oh, stop it!" ordered Wash, picking up one in each large hand by the scruff of the neck and tossing them out of his path as he strode from the room.

"And don't let me hear any more of such expressions from you," ordered their mother. She stepped to a bellpull. "I do not understand why Mrs. Umney has not attended to this."

Her summons was answered by a young parlourmaid whose auburn-haired radiance seemed to set the room aglow as she entered. An absolute stunner, she was. Mrs. Otis looked at her with benevolent surprise. Minister Otis's grumpy expression smoothed into one of robust pleasure. Miss Virginia took her in with the generous admiration that only a girl who was unconscious of her own beauty could have managed. Even the twins stopped kicking each other to take a look.

"Did you ring, ma'am?"

"Yes. Are you—"

"I am Sheila, ma'am," said the girl, curtseying prettily. "Bridget and I came early this morning—Bridget's the other new parlourmaid, ma'am."

"Ah, yes. I thought I heard a cart arrive quite early." Like Lady Canterville, Mrs. Otis found our birds troublesome in the morning, and was often awakened early. She smiled pleasantly at the new maid and added, "You're very pretty, Sheila."

"Thank you, ma'am," said Sheila, with another curtsey, and without losing her composure. Most parlourmaids would have answered with a simper and some silly remark.

"You speak quite well, too," said Mrs. Otis.

"Thank you, ma'am. I had the advantage of some education before my poor dear father lost his tailor shop and died of consumption, leaving us to make our own way as best we could."

"What a sad story. Well, I hope you will be happy with us, Sheila."

"Oh, thank you, ma'am. I'm sure I will be," said Sheila, smiling for the first time. I am certain that anyone outside would have been startled to see the stained-glass window suddenly light up.

"Good. Now, then, Sheila, which of you tidied up the room this morning?"

"I did, ma'am," said Sheila, and her brown eyes went with quick intelligence to the stain the Otises had been discussing. "If it's that bloodstain you're wondering about, ma'am, Mrs. Umney told me I was not to touch it on any account, as it could not be removed."

"I see. Very well, you may go," said Mrs. Otis, and after another quick and graceful curtsey, Sheila went toward the door just as young Washington returned. He glanced at her and then, as she slipped past him with modestly downcast eyes, blinked as though he had momentarily lost control of his eyeballs. It took him a moment to recover himself and pretend he had not been knocked for a loop.

"Who was that?" he asked with overdone casualness.

"One of the new maids, dear," said his mother.

"Oh." Shaking his head as though to clear it, Wash produced that infernal black stick of his and advanced on the stain.

"Now we shall see," he said, throwing a challenging glance at his father. Stooping, he went to work on the stain for a second time. And for a second time he removed it without leaving a trace, whilst I sat by glaring at him helplessly. His smugness, as he straightened up, was intolerable.

"There! You see?"

"Hmp!" His father tried not to sound impressed. "That's all fine and dandy, but . . . well, we'll see."

The following morning the stain had again appeared, and was again rubbed out by Washington.

"I tell you, it must be the ghost!" he insisted. "There can be no other explanation."

That night Minister Otis personally locked up the library and carried the key with him to his bedchamber. The third morning, however, the stain was back again. At that point even Minister Otis began to have second thoughts.

"Maybe the feller is around, after all."

"I'm sure of it, Pa. I'm going to write Myers and Podmore a letter about this," said Wash, and he went to work with his black stick.

"How interesting," said Mrs. Otis, looking on. "I have toyed with the idea in the past of joining the Psychical Society. Now I think I shall do so."

Also looking on, I vowed vengeance for the violence being done our sacred bloodstain; and that night, as Mr.

Oscar Wilde put it in one of his finer sentences, "all doubts about the objective existence of phantasmata were removed forever."

The balance of that day was a busy one for me. There was so much to think about. Everything had to be right.

A good deal of my time was spent not in the Tapestry Chamber but elsewhere. Like most highly cerebral types, I had my favourite secluded spots for various kinds of intense concentration. The Tapestry Chamber was fine for run-of-the-mill deductive reasoning, but for the heavy stuff, when I had a bit of haunting to do and wished to start my plans running along truly ingenious lines, it was to another region I repaired. At such times I loved to go down, down, down into a grim section of the ancient wing, the castle section of Canterville Chase, and slip into a certain dungeon cell that none but I had visited for well over three hundred years.

Of course, any well-appointed dwelling of the nobility, such as Canterville Chase, was liberally stocked with dungeon cells. I could have made my choice of several. The peculiar charm of this one, however, was that it was occupied. Well, at any rate, *had* been. Signs of occupancy were unmistakable.

As Oscar put it, "Imbedded in the wall was a huge iron ring, and chained to it was a gaunt skeleton, that was stretched out full length on the stone floor. It seemed to be trying to grasp with its long fleshless fingers an old-fashioned trencher and ewer, that were placed just out of reach. The jug had evidently once been filled with water, as it was covered inside with green mould. There was nothing on the trencher but a pile of dust."

A melancholy sight, to be sure.

Those bones had formerly belonged to one Robin Clump, a fletcher who lived in the village of Canterville Coomb during the time of Good Sir Alfred. One day Robin failed to pull his forelock when his lord rode by, or sold him a quiver of arrows with faulty feathers, or committed some other such heinous misdemeanour—the old nobleman was a stickler for manners, and a shrewd judge of arrows. At any rate, Sir Alfred, who had what I believe is called a "short fuse" today, was properly incensed.

"Getting above himself, is he? Fellow needs to be taught some manners!" decided the patriarchal disciplinarian, and he forthwith had Robin fetched off to the castle and down to the dungeon, where under his lordship's energetic direction Robin was made comfortable in the manner described by Oscar.

"A couple of weeks in there and he'll think twice next time before he lets me ride past without so much as a decent grovel!" said the beloved lord, or perhaps, "Next time he won't try to pawn off any half-fledged arrows on *me*!"

Tenderhearted man that he was, Sir Alfred only meant to teach the fellow an object lesson and release him as soon as the point had been driven home. But then, a man of affairs such as the first earl had many things on his mind—boar hunts and masked balls, hanging of felons and burning of heretics at the stake, conspiracies against the Crown, seduction of the comelier village wenches—people today have no idea how busy manor life was then—and what with one thing and another poor Robin Clump completely slipped his mind. It was only when, a year or so later, he had occasion to sentence another member of the Clump family to be whipped and branded for looking at a pheasant as though he might be thinking of snaring it that the saintly nobleman remembered him.

"Robin Clump!" he cried, smiting his brow. Then he sighed and shrugged. "Well, it's too late now."

Thus it was that Robin had lain there mouldering away for three centuries and more, with never a visitor except myself. Yet his involuntary sacrifice had not been in vain, for I found him always to be an inspiration when I was trying to solve some especially knotty problem. On this occasion it was my final choice of costume that was at stake. It took me quite a while to decide, sitting there on a discarded headman's block which had once supported a bowl of fresh fruit cunningly arranged as an additional torment to the starving man, but finally I had it. Chuckling happily, I left young Clump and returned to the Tapestry Chamber to rummage through my wardrobe.

By now the stables had been provided with a good team of bays, two grooms, a coachman, and a carriage, and in the cool of the evening the Otis family went for a drive. Returning at nine o'clock, they had a light supper, spent the evening in conversation, and retired at eleven o'clock. Within half an hour, all the lamps were out.

The stage was set.

At such a moment as this it is hard to avoid metaphors of a theatrical nature. In the Tapestry Chamber, where Lady Eleanore was assisting me in the role of wardrobe mistress and dresser, the atmosphere was that of a star's dressing room on opening night. The same electrically charged atmosphere, the same excitement and tension. All that was lacking were flowers and telegrams.

"Do I have my eyebrows right?" I asked anxiously, peering into the glass above my dressing table. Lady Eleanore gave my work a critical inspection.

"Too level. The right one should be cocked up half an

inch more," she said, and I carefully followed her instructions, having found her to be a first-class judge of visual effects both facial and sartorial. To be sure, she had always had a sense of style, and since she looked well in basic black, her own appearance was quite smart now. This time she had, of course, shed her homely guise as Mrs. Umney and resumed her own form, so that now she was again the young woman she had been at the time of her final bit of needlework. And my normal appearance, of course, was what it had been on the night I vanished under such mysterious circumstances.

Tonight, however, Lady Eleanore's looks seemed subtly enhanced.

"Elly," I said, giving her a keen glance in the mirror, "you know, you're getting better looking every century. What have you been doing to yourself?"

She had the conscience to blush, producing a pinkness that became her.

"Well, as a witch I *am* allowed a certain latitude," she said, "but over and above that I must confess that since the Otises arrived I—well, I had a woman's natural curiosity about such things . . ."

"What things?"

"Mrs. Otis's things. She has a large collection of beauty aids. I had a chance to examine them, and one jar—well, the claims made on its label tempted me to try it."

"Oh? And which one was that?"

"Beaton's Beneficent Beautifying Balm."

"You mean you've been using it?"

"Yes."

"Does Mrs. Otis know this?"

"Of course not."

"Well, really, Eleanore, I *am* surprised. Pilfering!"

"Look who's talking."

"Oh, come off it! Just because I may have held out a few payments on Sbagliorone—"

"A few? All of them!"

"—and deprived a rascally Ponte Vecchian of the pleasure of overcharging me for a silly stiletto—"

"Where is that thing now?"

"In the British Museum, I believe—is no excuse for your pinching Mrs. Otis's cosmetics!" I concluded sternly. By now her cheeks were quite rosy, and I found myself stopping to take another look at her. "Still and all, it seems to be doing more for you than it does for her, and *she's* not bad-looking."

I turned back to my dressing table, almost embarrassed by my own tribute, but our eyes met in the glass. She had lifted her hand as though to touch me, but drew it away and let it fall to her side.

"Well, at any rate, it's a help to have you on the premises when there's something as serious as the Otises to be dealt with," I said, making a great show of getting back down to business with some black eye shadow. "How long do you plan to stay on this time?"

"Until our appointed tasks are accomplished."

"Not for long, eh?" I rejoined, laughing confidently, yet experiencing a curious little twinge of dissatisfaction. It was ridiculous, of course, but I very nearly felt as though this time, once I was again free of her company, I might almost miss her.

The fatal hour had come.

Terror stalked the corridors of Canterville Chase.

Slowly clanking my way along the polished boards, I stopped outside the Minister's chamber. The senior Otises

49

slept together in a large canopied bed. Mrs. Otis was inclined to sleep soundly until the birds began to tune up. The Minister, however, was a light sleeper. Whilst I waited, I enjoyed picturing how he must even now be sitting bolt upright in bed, his scalp crawling (unfortunately he had no hair left to stand on end), his brow bathed in a sudden prickle of cold perspiration, his breath shortening painfully. I gave my chains a couple more good clanks, and then the door opened, and there he was, in a nightshirt and purple dressing gown.

"Right in front of him," in Oscar's words, the Minister "saw, in the wan moonlight, an old man of terrible aspect. His eyes were as red as burning coals; long grey hair fell over his shoulders in matted coils; his garments, which were of antique cut, were soiled and ragged, and from his wrists and ankles hung heavy manacles and rusty gyves."

A sight, I felt, that should have set the family to packing their bags before cockcrow, provided Minister Otis's shattered condition made it safe to move him by that time. I expected him to utter a strangled cry as he flung a hand before his eyes to blot out the horrid sight, and to be struck down in a heap at my feet.

Instead, the man put his hand in his dressing gown pocket, brought out a small brown bottle, and thrust it at me with these words:

"My dear sir, I really must insist on your oiling those chains, and have brought you for that purpose a small bottle of the Tammany Rising Sun Lubricator. It is said to be completely efficacious upon one application, and there are several testimonials to that effect on the wrapper from some of our most eminent native divines. I shall leave it here for you by the bedroom candles, and will be happy to supply you with more should you require it."

And with this pompous peroration off his chest, the little red rooster of a man set the bottle on a marble-topped table, closed the door in my face, and retired to rest.

For an instant I stood there, a speechless spectre. After a three-century string of unbroken successes, to have a door closed in my face as if I were some panhandling indigent or a door-to-door salesman of inferior dust mops—it was monstrous! But then humiliation overwhelmed me. I snatched up the bottle and, as Oscar reported, I "fled down the corridor, uttering hollow groans, and emitting a ghastly green light." Well, who wouldn't, after an experience like that?

Yet there was worse to come. Just as I reached the top of the great oak staircase, the door of the Blue Bedchamber was flung open, two little gargoyles in nightshirts appeared, and a large pillow whizzed past my head!

Well, that did it. Hastily shifting gears, I thinned out and vanished through the wainscotting, thankful I had mastered the art at the Academy. Moments later I was once again in the Tapestry Chamber, trying to get my breath back, and staring with glazed eyes at the small brown bottle still clutched in my trembling hand.

Oscar would have it that in my indignation I dashed the bottle violently upon the floor, but that was untrue. Spread that lubricant gook all over our beautiful floors? I should hope not! I uncorked it and examined it, and marveled that several "eminent native divines" had written testimonials to the stuff. Setting it aside on my night table, I sprawled on the bed and gave myself up to black thoughts.

Never in three hundred years had I been so grossly insulted. When I thought back over all I had accomplished in that time, this setback seemed unbelievable.

That old dowager duchess of Bolton, as tough a customer as ever wore lace and diamonds—look at the job I had done on her! Now I wished heartily I had never gone near the old harridan; little had I guessed what a succession of disasters I was setting in motion with that lighthearted escapade! But what about other highlights in my career? Four housemaids in hysterics after I had merely grinned at them through a curtain. Reverend Augustus Dampier, our parish rector, still under treatment after a midnight encounter. Old Madame de Tremouillac, who gave up her acquaintance with Voltaire and went back to the Church after I had visited her as a skeleton. The beautiful Lady Stutfield, who "was always obliged to wear a black velvet band round her throat to hide the mark of five fingers burnt upon her white skin, and who drowned herself at last in the carp pond at the end of King's Walk." These and a dozen other artistic triumphs passed through my mind. And now, to be handed a bottle of Rising Sun Lubricator and narrowly miss concussion from a large pillow—had it come to that?

No! There would be a next time—and next time I would not fail!

SIX

THOSE ABOMINABLE AMERICANS had spoiled my evening, and were threatening to spoil my record. I had underestimated them badly. I saw now that I would have to go all out if I expected to rid Canterville Chase of their presence. The situation was serious. Naturally I would never have countenanced the sale of the house to the Otises had I not been confident I could frighten them away in short order. Now I felt like a luckless exterminator, who, after doing his best in an infested house, discovers that not only are the insect pests still in possession of the premises, but that his own clothes are full of fleas.

Certain I would be the chief topic of discussion at the breakfast table next morning, I thinned myself out thoroughly and hurried over to eavesdrop.

Nothing of what was said gave me any pleasure. Not a word was spoken by Minister Otis indicating the slightest aesthetic appreciation for costuming, lighting, sound effects, or performance. Instead, he contented himself with various patronizing remarks and some censure, far too slight, of the twins.

"I have no wish," he twanged, "to do the ghost any personal injury, and I must say that, considering the length of time he has been in the house, I don't think it is at all polite to throw pillows at him"—a very just remark, at which, I am sorry to say, the twins burst into shouts of laughter. "Upon the other hand," he continued, "if he really declines to use the Rising Sun Lubricator, we shall have to take his chains from him. It would be quite impossible to sleep, with such a noise going on outside the bedrooms."

A threat! A ruddy threat! The little rooster sat there blandly talking about taking my chains away from me, as though I were part of the household staff! It was all I could do not to firm up, seize the marmalade pot, and empty it on his shiny bald head. Rather than spend another moment in his provoking presence, I whirled away into the library to recover my composure.

Here I found something more pleasant to rest my eyes upon. Moving about competently with cloth and duster, the parlourmaid Sheila was tidying up the room. Settling myself in my accustomed place I observed with pleasure the lissome grace of her slender form, the sensuous curves of her slim hips, the provocative rise and fall of her pert bosom. I had thought they no longer made serving wenches the way they used to, but young Sheila changed my mind. She looked to be about eighteen, and I was just wishing I were three hundred years younger myself when who should come sidling into the library, trying to look as if he had just happened along, but young Washington Otis.

His pathetic attempt to act nonchalant was marred by the manner in which he changed colour, gulped, and ran a finger round his collar as though it were strangling him.

"Oh! Good morning, Sheila!" he croaked.

She gave him a brief glance and dropped him a quick curtsey that barely interrupted her domestic activities.

"Good morning, sir."

With awkward strides he moved nearer, his approach observed out of the corner of one glinting brown eye as Sheila continued her dusting. Licking his lips, he attempted a devil-may-care chuckle.

"You're a bonny young lass, Sheila!"

What an awful line! Now I saw it all. The poor simp had been boning up on novels about English country life in the good old days, novels in which the young lord of the manor was constantly pursuing parlourmaids whenever they took his fancy; and Wash had decided to have a go at it.

Sighing, Sheila turned and faced him.

"Am I, sir?" she asked in a cool voice which should have warned him off, except that Wash was too far committed to stop himself now.

"You are indeed! Give us a k-kiss, eh?" he stammered, and made a fumbling grab for her.

The smack that sent him reeling back left one of his cheeks even redder than the other, which was quite an accomplishment.

"I am a maid, sir, and I intend to remain one," said Sheila, and she left him watching her exit with his hand on his flaming cheek.

Now, if such a thing had taken place in one of those novels he had been reading, the offending parlourmaid would have left the young lord gnashing his teeth and vowing a terrible vengeance on her, but here Wash missed his way. Instead, his punch-drunk gaze followed her with absolute adoration. An instant later Miss Virginia came through the doorway, glancing back in the direction Sheila had gone. Finding her brother present, she gave him a quick appraisal that was shrewd beyond her years.

"Wash, what happened to your face?"

"What? Oh, I—er—stumbled against the—"

"You did not. Sheila smacked it!"

Wash glared helplessly at his sister, but then his glare dissolved into agony.

"Well, what if she did? She's the purest, loveliest creature I've ever seen, and I'm not fit to touch the hem of her garment!" he moaned with the extravagance of his tender years.

His sister pounced.

"You're in love with her!"

"I adore her!"

"Oh, good! I'm glad, because I did so need a hold on you! I won't say a word about it, Wash—but now you must help *me*!"

Poor Wash was already biting his tongue, but it was too late. He eyed her warily.

"What are you talking about?"

"Well, Cecil can't very well invite *himself* here, can he? His nasty old guardians wouldn't let him, anyway—and *I* can't ask Mama to ask him, because she'd ask a lot of questions about why I wanted to ask him, and wouldn't ask him —but *you* could ask her to ask him and she'd ask him."

Wash picked his way through all these askings and then stared at her.

"Cecil? You mean that little duke of Cheshire?"

"He's not little! He's almost as tall as you are!"

"But—why, he's barely eighteen—"

"He *is* eighteen, going on nineteen—I looked him up in *Burke's Peerage*!"

"Don't tell me you've fallen for *him*!"

"Certainly not," said Virginia with head-tossing dignity.

"I—I just want to see him again. If you'd tell Mama you thought he was nice, and you'd like to know him better, she'd invite him down in a minute!"

"For pity's sake, Ginny, I hardly know the fellow! I only saw him once, when you had that silly race with old Lord Bilton up in London, and I didn't speak more than six words to him then!"

"That doesn't matter."

"Besides, the little ass proposed to you."

"How dare you call him names!"

"Well, he did."

"But that was only—it was only high spirits. Wash, you're being impossible. If you'd rather I told Mama—"

"You be quiet!"

"Oh, Wash, do be a dear, good brother! There's nothing to worry about. Papa and Mama don't know anything about what happened in London, so they won't be alarmed. . . ."

If it were not for Lady Eleanore I might have found this conversation mystifying, but thanks to her I could grasp it. Even Oscar was privy to the incident mentioned in their discussion, and reported it in his account. Miss Virginia, he said, "had once raced old Lord Bilton on her pony twice round the park, winning by a length and a half, just in front of the Achilles statue, to the huge delight of the young duke of Cheshire, who proposed to her on the spot, and was sent back to Eton that very night by his guardians, in floods of tears." The way Lady Eleanore learned about the episode was from Miss Virginia herself. Since coming to Canterville Chase, the girl had quickly grown fond of Mrs. Umney and had made her a confidante in many matters.

"I'll patch things up for you with Sheila, you see if I don't!" promised Virginia, and of course in the end she bent poor Wash to her will—which, one was rapidly coming to see, was a will of iron. Miss Virginia Otis would, I decided then and there, bear watching.

Perhaps you are expecting to hear that the very next night I mounted a new campaign, as some headstrong novice might have done. No, a thing one learns as a ghost is that there is plenty of time. For that matter, perhaps the sensible course would have been simply to retire to the Tapestry Chamber and wait them out. I could have won that game hands down—but that would have been too easy. Such was not my temperament. As the fourth Lord Canterville (1546–1584), I had always been a man of action, and ever since then I had been a ghost of action. Long before the Otises' arrival I had had enough of sitting around in an empty house thumbing through old issues of the *Cornhill Magazine* or rereading the poetry of Mrs. Hemans while the family was away. A monotonous existence had left me thoroughly discontented; I was spoiling for action; but at the same time there was no point in allowing myself to be precipitated into hasty and ill-conceived counteroffensives. One should meditate, organize, and then—strike!

For the rest of the week, then, the Otises were undisturbed. The only thing that excited any attention was the continual renewal of the bloodstain on the library floor, and that principally because of the spectacular mutations of the colour. Some mornings it was found to be a dull red, on others vermillion or a rich purple, and on one occasion a bright emerald green. Being the sort of people they were, the Otises took all this as a form of amusement, and even made bets each evening as to what colour would show up next morning. Only Miss Virginia had the good taste to look distressed at the sight, and even seemed on the point of tears the morning it was emerald green. I must confess it became harder and harder to put her in the same category with the rest of the family.

What the effort cost me to maintain that bloodstain I shall not even go into. For me it became almost a patriotic gesture, like keeping the flag flying. There'll always be an England, and an English bloodstain—that sort of thing. Each morning that young fanatic Wash went down on his hands and knees to attack the stain with his vicious Paragon Detergent, and each morning I stood invisibly by, tantalized by his position, longing to kick him in the pants. One morning I actually did, but being thinned out to invisibility, my foot did not register on his behind.

Each time he rose to his feet, having eradicated yet another bloodstain, his gushing remarks about the Paragon Detergent resembled those to be heard on your telly concerning your present-day detergents. If Washington Otis were with us now he would probably be seen standing between two credulous housewives saying, "Now, ladies, which do you think is Pinkerton's and which is Brand X?"

He had just gone down on his knees one morning to begin his daily desecration, alone in the library except for myself, when Sheila entered right center to retrieve a polishing cloth she had left on the mantelpiece.

"Oh, I'm sorry, sir," she said, as Wash turned redder than the original stain and scrambled to his feet.

"It's all right, S-Sheila, I—er—"

"I wish I could do that for you, sir, since I am charged with keeping this room in order. Mrs. Umney provides some very good scouring powder—"

"Oh, I wouldn't think of asking you to—er—I'm only too glad to—uh— Besides, I don't believe you would find an ordinary scouring powder as effective as Pinkerton's Detergent," he said, holding up his favorite weapon and drawing courage from it.

"Very well, sir."

They stood looking at each other for the five awkward seconds it took Wash to bring himself to further speech. He cleared his throat in a manner that suggested a golf ball had somehow become lodged in it.

"Er—Sheila, I want to apologize for my boorish actions the other morning."

A curious sparkle illumined her bright brown eyes for an instant before lovely long lashes lowered to hide them briefly from his dazzled view.

"That's quite all right, sir. It was gentlemanly of you not to attempt some mean revenge on me, and to keep the matter private between us."

"Well, not exactly private," said Wash, dropping his voice. "My sister caught on, and she's using her knowledge to blackmail me!"

"Blackmail?" Sheila's eyes widened in a startled glance. "She doesn't seem that kind at all. How—"

"She agreed not to say anything about it to—to anybody if I'd ask Mother to invite the duke of Cheshire down for a visit."

"You mean, the young gentleman who proposed to her when she—"

"You know about it!"

"Mrs. Umney told me—in strictest confidence, of course."

"Well, I'll be switched!" said Wash, pleased at finding himself on similarly confidential terms with Sheila.

"It's humiliating to think that a young woman such as your sister should have to resort to such subterfuges in order to accomplish a perfectly innocent end," said Sheila indignantly.

"Well, I don't know how innocent," said Wash. "I think she's smitten with him."

"Nevertheless . . ."

"At any rate, I asked Mother, and she invited him, and he's coming."

"I see," said Sheila, her mind still obviously preoccupied with brooding on injustice. "Mr. Otis, have you read the works of your countrywoman Mrs. Amelia Bloomer?"

Now here was a name that all red-blooded American males of that day greeted with hoots of derisive laughter; but such was Wash's infatuation that he actually kept his face straight and looked at her with earnest attention.

"Well, no, I can't say as I have," he admitted.

"You should, sir. She is a wonderful woman. In fact, you have many outstanding figures in the women's rights movement in America—Mrs. Bloomer, Miss Susan B. Anthony, and others. Mrs. Bloomer's writings first appeared in her magazine, *The Lily*. I'm only sorry *The Lily* ceased publication before I was born."

"It's a shame!" agreed Wash—he was ready, of course, to agree with anything.

"I have some of her tracts with me, if you would care to read them, sir."

"Oh, I would, I would! I'll meet you here again tomorrow, right after breakfast, and you can give them to me."

"Thank you, sir. And now, if you would like to get back to that bloodstain, sir, I won't bother you. I must return to the servants' hall." She glanced down at the stain. "Isn't it strange, the way it changes colour? It must have something to do with that detergent you use."

"I'm sure that's it!" agreed Wash.

Taking her polishing cloth from the mantelpiece, Sheila dropped him a curtsey, gave him a smile that left him staggering blissfully, and withdrew.

I won't deny that I watched the whole of this scene with malicious enjoyment, anticipating the paternal ire that would be aroused once Minister Otis learned his son had become involved with a parlourmaid. The fact that the Minister was a Democrat did not mean he was democratic, and furthermore he was a devout descendant of his Puritan ancestors. I left Wash standing there in his trance and turned my attention to more serious matters.

That was a dreadful week. To be honest, I was suffering from ghost's gripe. You have heard of writer's block, that condition of mind in which a writer can't think of anything to write about? Well, my condition was just the opposite. I could think of too *many* possibilities in my line. I mooned around, and the first thing I knew it was Sunday night and another week down the drain.

Early that evening Lady Eleanore dropped by. She had more free time now, since after that first dinner Mrs. Otis had hastily hired a cook and paid the woman extra to come immediately to the rescue. Obviously intending only a brief visit, Lady Eleanore had not bothered to change from her aged-housekeeper disguise.

"I bid you welcome to the Tapestry Chamber, Goodwife Umney," I said, mimicking that antique folderol with which she had creakily greeted the Otises on the day of their arrival. "I'm glad you dropped by. I'm having a lot of trouble choosing the role in which to make my come-back."

"How about Martin o' the Marsh, or the Mangled Minstrel?"

"I doubt that this bunch have any ear for music."

"Queasy Quentin, or the Disembowelled Corpse?"

"Wash would probably whip out a medical book and start talking about the evils of unsuccessful surgery."

"Griswold the Gory?"

"Stop reminding me of blood! It hasn't been a marked success around here."

"Well, at any rate, I wish you'd get cracking again, and soon."

"Don't rush me. There is plenty of time."

"Not for me, there isn't. I need some quick relief. Cook's been took with a fever, as she puts it, and I've had to put on the apron again."

"Oh, that's it, is it? Well, in that case, I can rest on my oars. You should be able to whip up something that will clear Canterville Chase of the Otises in a twinkling!"

"No, that wouldn't be fair. We have to play by the rules, and this is your show. *You're* supposed to do the job."

"You mean, you can't even lend a helping hand now and then?"

"Oh, a change of weather, thunder and lightning as needed, that sort of thing—but otherwise, no."

The burdens of state sat heavily on my shoulders, but after a moment I squared those shoulders, and my face took on the same British bulldog look that would stand Sir Winston Churchill in good stead when he copied it over half a century later.

"We shall fight on the beaches, we shall fight on the landing grounds, we shall fight in the fields and in the streets, we shall fight in the hills; we shall never surrender," I growled, eerily foreshadowing the very words he would utter himself on a subsequent occasion.

And for both of us, at the time we spoke those words, the worst was still ahead.

seven

M Y NEW TRIALS began that very night. When all was still in the house, I quietly paced the corridors, trying to get a new idea. In an unlucky moment in the great entrance hall, my own suit of armour caught my eye. As Oscar pointed out, I "had worn it with success at the Kenilworth tournament, and had been highly complimented on it by no less a person than the Virgin Queen herself." Impulsively I lifted off the breastplate, intending to slip it on just to have a look at myself in it, hoping it might lead me to some inspiration.

If I have a shortcoming, it is that I am sometimes absent-minded. A fearful crash was heard in the great entrance hall, bringing a rush of male Otises out into the upper hall and down the stairs. There they found the breastplate on the floor and the Canterville Ghost sitting in a high-backed chair rubbing his knees and cursing in agony. I had forgotten to firm myself up to anything like the necessary pitch, and the weight of that fool breastplate had toppled me over onto the flagstone floor, skinning both of my knees and the knuckles of my right hand.

Minister Otis was armed with a large Colt revolver, the twins with peashooters.

"Coo! It's Im again!" cried the twins, and they simultaneously pitted my forehead with direct hits.

For once Oscar was quite factual when he wrote that "the ghost started up with a wild shriek of rage, and swept through them like a mist, extinguishing Washington Otis's candle as he passed, and so leaving them all in total darkness." Drastic measures were in order. By the time I had reached the top of the staircase I had decided to spare them nothing. I would subject them to my celebrated peal of demoniac laughter!

"Hahahahahahahahahahahahahahahaha . . . !"

The Canterville laugh, that cornucopia of shrieks, gibbers, belches, retches, and rumbles, rang again and again from the old vaulted roof. The final echo was still bouncing around when the nearby bedchamber door opened and Mrs. Otis came out in a light blue dressing gown and carrying a candle, as though she were about to do Lady Macbeth's sleepwalking scene. She spoke, however, in her usual calm cadences as she handed me a small bottle.

"I am afraid you are far from well," she said, "and have brought you a bottle of Doctor Dobell's tincture. If it is indigestion, you will find it a most excellent remedy."

I vanished with a deep churchyard groan.

We Cantervilles bounce back, however. Ruthlessly determined now, I put together an outfit that Lady Eleanore, an exacting critic, had to agree was a brilliant choice. When we had finished she held me off at arm's length and surveyed me proudly.

"Simon, you have never looked more revolting!" Her compliment pleased me so inordinately I blushed like a schoolgirl. "And that's saying something," she added, causing me almost to strut as I walked toward a full-length mirror to admire myself.

"Splendid! But Elly, it's your little touches that make it," I declared generously. "The jagged rib bone peeping through a tear in the winding-sheet, the hint of leprous skin folded out over the neck-frill, the blotch of something nauseously suggestive on the hem of the garment— My dear, I don't know what I'd do without you."

I was filled with new confidence. To date, as I saw it, my failures could be laid at the door of a simple tactical error: a neglect of the horrible. Gyves and chains and manacles are all very well, but they tend to make one more an object of pity than of frightfulness. And in my second, accidental appearance, of course, I had simply been a figure of fun, a poor lout rubbing his skinned knees. Small wonder the Otises had not yet taken me seriously. Well, if it was the grisly and the gruesome they required to bring them down, then they would have it! No more Mr. Nice Guy!

When the hoary grandfather's clock in the great entrance hall tolled the doleful hour of midnight, I set forth to accomplish my fell purpose. Nearing the passage that led to the Otises' bedrooms, I paused, then turned the corner.

As I did so a flash of lightning revealed a macabre sight that tore a scream from my lips.

In that instant every detail seared itself into my mind: the bald, burnished head; the round, fat, maggoty-white face; the eyes burning with scarlet light; the hellfire mouth; the winding-sheet like my own but hideous in its dead-whiteness; the glittering falchion held aloft; and the placard with antique lettering on the cavernous breast. Then blackness blotted out all.

Never having seen a ghost before, I was scared out of

my wits. Spinning four feet into the air, I lit running and never stopped till I was back in my own bed with the bed-clothes over my head.

It took hours for indignation to quell terror—who was this bold intruder, and what was he doing in my territory? —and for practical considerations to supplant indignation— why not join forces and really do a job on the Otis family? It was nearly daylight before I made my brave return to the upstairs corridor—only to find a collapsed ghost lying at my feet! A white dimity bed curtain, a broom, a kitchen cleaver, and a hollow turnip! Staring at the placard, which was still hanging on the confounded japery, I read words that churned my bowels:

ꙮ𝔢 ꙮ𝔱𝔦𝔰 𝔊𝔥𝔬𝔰𝔱𝔢
ꙮ𝔢 ꙮnlie 𝔗rue and ꙮriginale 𝔖pooke
𝔅eware of ꙮ𝔢 𝔍mitationes
𝔄ll others are 𝔠ounterfeite

After that shattering experience, Oscar claimed that I "retired to a comfortable lead coffin, and stayed there till evening." What nonsense! I think he must have had me confused with that old fraud Count Dracula. The fact is that once I had regained the Tapestry Chamber, I picked up a spoon and went to my night table.

If Mrs. Otis's description of the stuff was at all accurate, Dr. Dobell's tincture was just what I needed.

Another mistake.

Whatever I needed, it certainly wasn't Dr. Dobell. After several bad sessions in the loo, I had just crawled back into bed, weak as a kitten, when there came a rap at the door.

Through some arcane means of her own, Lady Eleanore had learned of my condition.

"Come!" I groaned, and turned a face flushed with shame toward the wall. Lady Eleanore slipped in carrying a large steaming bowl and a spoon. She approached the bedside.

"Here's what my boy needs," she crooned, "some nice chicken soup!"

My stomach rumbled alarmingly, and I twisted my head around to glare at her.

"For pity's sake, Elly, after the agony I've gone through, I couldn't possibly keep a thing on my stomach! Oh, if I only knew where that Doctor Dobell is, I'd give him such a haunting!"

Setting the bowl on my night table, she dipped out a spoonful of soup.

"So try a little."

And, of course, she was right. I not only kept the soup down, it tasted good. Soon I was resting more comfortably and feeling up to addressing my new grievances.

"Elly, surely by now you must realise those little fiends are no ordinary adversaries! Have you checked them out? Are you sure they're not a pair of poltergeists on special assignment?"

She shook her head pityingly.

"No, Simon, you must face it. You are dealing with a pair of ordinary American boys."

I rolled weakly onto my back with a heartfelt cry.

"God help America!"

But then the spasm of despair passed, and I began to think of Alfred the Great and Robert Bruce, and of John Paul Jones saying, "I have not yet begun to fight," and the good old Canterville courage began to revive.

"Well, never mind. What's one more little setback? This one hardly counts, anyway, since no one even saw me. I'll lie low for a time, and when next I strike, it shall be for keeps!"

"That's the way to talk!"

"It's that chicken soup. It's done wonders for me. I almost feel like getting up!"

Lady Eleanore beamed.

"My cooking is improving, isn't it? I made it myself."

"You didn't!"

"I did."

"Amazing! It's black magic, that's what it is!"

She frowned.

"Please, Simon. Don't blaspheme." Then her expression softened again, and she sighed.

"What's the matter?"

Her fine eyes brooded into space.

"Oh, I was just thinking. . . . Why couldn't we learn anything when we were young? Why couldn't we understand what was really important? A few kind words, a little appreciation of the things I *did* do well, might have made me a completely other wife to you. . . ."

"And a softer tongue on your part might have made me another husband. Yes, the thought has occurred to me, too, here of late. . . . But still, let's give the past its due. It wasn't all bad. Remember that night on our honeymoon, in Venice—"

"When we filled ourselves with spaghetti *alle vongole* and that good Soave wine—"

"Oceans of it!"

"—and then got into a gondola with that nice gondolier who never tried to peek at us but simply sang and sang . . . ?"

"What a night!" I sighed, aglow with memories. "Oh, Elly, can we ever be like that again?"

"I hardly think so."

"Come now, is there no chance at all? Couldn't there be, say, a special dispensation . . . ?"

She laughed briefly.

"I've heard of some pretty special ones, but nothing quite like that!"

I lay back on my pillow, a disappointed dreamer. "Pity. Still, next time you come, do me a favour."

"What?"

"Bring more chicken soup. It's worth a try!"

eight

FOR SEVERAL DAYS I stayed put, rethinking my strategy. For one thing, I decided that from then on I would deny them the famous bloodstain. None of the Otises had shown any aesthetic appreciation of it, and that detergent freak would not let it alone. So they could just jolly well do without.

There were my duties to be considered, of course. Every ghost is expected to do his duty, and I was not one to neglect mine. But don't think it was easy! On Wednesday night I crept up to the large oriel window for my biweekly gibber—and twice was sent sprawling over strings stretched across dark passageways. Then on Saturday night, having waited till the wee hours to attempt a quick and stealthy tour of the corridors, I stepped out of my room and soared off the top step of the back staircase like a ski-jumper off the slide at Innsbruck, except that mine was a butter slide! It was all I could do to rise and limp slowly up the stairs to my chamber.

All this added fuel to the fire, of course.

I was again laid up for several days, and I don't know when I might have recovered had it not been for a special ointment Lady Eleanore brewed up for me—some mixture of eye of newt, toe of frog, wool of bat, tongue of dog, and other salubrious ingredients from an old recipe.

"Elly, those rotten kids are getting too close for comfort," I fretted as she rubbed ointment on my battered limbs one evening. "That butter slide shows they're hot on my trail. It's only a question of time till they fathom the secret of my door. The next thing I know they'll be paying *me* midnight visits! In fact, I've been doing a lot of thinking, lying here, and I'm beginning to see where I went wrong. I overplayed my hand. I tried to take on the whole Otis clan at once, instead of picking them off one at a time. Rather than spread myself thin, what I've got to do is concentrate on my worst enemies."

"You mean the twins?"

"Who else?"

"One at a time?"

"In their case I'll try for two. And this time I intend to go all out. No holds barred."

"Simon! You don't mean . . ."

"Yes."

"Not—"

"Yes. Reckless Rupert, or the Headless Earl."

She gasped.

"Simon, do you think that is wise? Remember what it did to Lady Barbara Modish, and she was an Englishwoman who was *used* to apparitions. What if those boys perished from fright? A thing like that could be very bad for Anglo-American relations, and just now we need their trade."

"Well, that's just too bad. Our revered prime minister, Mr. Gladstone, will have to straighten things out as best he can. Besides, I'm not worried about that. I may reduce the twins to a pair of drooling imbeciles, but as far as their perishing from anything this side of the Final Trump is concerned, I am sure they are indestructible. The Four Horsemen of the Apocalypse themselves would find their hands full with those two."

"Well, all right, Simon. If your mind is made up, we'll do it, but I hate to think of the job we've got ahead of us. It will take a good three hours to get you into that costume."

"If a thing is worth doing, it's worth doing well," I countered. "You'll see, it will be worth every minute we spend on it!"

It was more than seventy years since I had last appeared in my most celebrated disguise and given Babs Modish such a fright, so our task was every bit as difficult and time-consuming as Lady Eleanore had anticipated. I had to hunt everywhere for the big leather riding boots, and when I found them they seemed a trifle large.

"I think I must have put the wrong boot trees in these the last time I packed them away. What's more, I can only find one of the horse pistols," I said, rummaging through an old steamer trunk. "I'm positive I put both of them in here when I—"

"Simon, *why* don't you take an inventory of your things?" scolded Lady Eleanore. "I've told you again and again—"

"I know, I know, but never mind that now—I can make do with one pistol. Can't hold them both and the head as well, anyway."

On the whole I was well pleased with my appearance, especially once I had added Reckless Rupert's head. Oscar was under the impression that it was not included among my accessories. Why, it was the crowning touch of my costume! Well, no, *crowning* is hardly the right word, to be sure; but tucked under my arm with eyes ablaze and tongue slavering from open mouth, while my own head was concealed beneath the bloody stub of a neck, Rupert's head was the sort of sartorial accent that captures attention. All in all, I felt complete confidence as I trod the boards that night.

The midnight hour found me stalking down the upstairs corridor toward the Blue Bedchamber, which was the one occupied by my prey. There, to make my errand all the easier, I found the door standing slightly ajar. With a dramatic gesture I flung it open and stepped inside.

Stifled shrieks from the four-poster bed—shrieks of laughter—reached my horrified ears at the same instant a heavy jug of water plummeted down on me, wetting me to the skin and giving poor Rupert's head a soaking equaled only by the duke of Clarence's when he was drowned head-first in a butt of malmsey. Which, of course, made the thing slippery and hard to hold onto, especially for a ghost who was already as upset and distraught as I was.

The result was that as I raced away down the corridor, clawing open the shirtwaist in front of my eyes in order to see better where I was going, his lordship's head slipped from under my arm like a fumbled football and went rolling away down the corridor just when I was planning to vanish into the wainscotting. As I stopped and watched, it hooked round a corner and went bumping away down a flight of stairs.

Uttering a curse I won't sully your ears with, I turned to pursue it, leaving behind a trail of puddles with every step I took. After a few strides, I cast one of those oversized riding boots like a horse casting a shoe. It went flying to one side and nearly smashed a marble bust of Cato the Elder. I could not leave it behind, so I had to stop and retrieve it. Then, with riding boot in one hand and horse pistol in the other, I hop-skipped along the corridor and rushed down the stairs two at a time.

When I reached the broad hallway at the bottom, the head was nowhere to be seen. It had vanished.

I peered under a massive old bookcase that stood against a wall, but apart from dust and cobwebs there was nothing beneath it. Before I could search further, the patter of little feet in the corridor above sent a new chill through my already chilled frame. The monsters were coming!

With a final curse I rose and vanished through the wainscotting and retreated to my room with a new worry piled atop all my others. Where was that beastly head?

By the time Lady Eleanore arrived with chicken soup, I was already in bed and sneezing.

"I heard the commotion," she said, putting the bowl on my night table and settling herself to minister. "What happened this time?"

I gave her a moving account of this latest atrocity. As she listened, the corners of her mouth began to twitch, and finally she threw back her head and laughed till she had to wipe away the tears.

"Oh, Simon! To think you'd fall for that one! Ah, those twins! If ever they do want to break into the poltergeist field, I shall certainly put in a word for them."

I glared at her helplessly.

"You may laugh all you wish, but I was soaked to the ectoplasm and my costume is ruined! Look at it! It will take a century to get it put right again, even if we send it out!"

"Oh, don't be silly." She examined the rumpled heap of finery on the floor. "I'll take care of it."

"Very well. But you haven't heard all. There's worse to come. I lost my head!"

"It certainly sounds like it."

"No, no, goose, I mean Reckless Rupert's head!"

I can assure you *that* wiped the smile from the minx's face. In the midst of preparing to transfer soup into me she paused, transfixed, and gazed at me wide-eyed.

"The . . . Headless . . . Earl's . . . head?"

"Yes!"

"Oh, really, Simon! How could you be so careless?"

"*You* try carrying a wet head under your arm and you won't be so critical! Do you have any idea how heavy your average head is? Weighs a ton! And Reckless Rupert's is bigger than average. He took a size eight-and-a-quarter hat, in the days when he was still taking hats."

"But, Simon, *where* did you lose it?"

I described the circumstances.

"When I got down there it was simply nowhere to be seen. I looked under the bookcase, but it wasn't there. Incidentally, you'd better get after those housemaids of yours, they're loafing on the job." I was in a frame of mind where any petty opportunity to criticize was welcome. "They haven't swept under there in ages."

"Oh, for pity's sake, Simon!"

"Well, you're supposed to be the housekeeper," I muttered in a sulky voice, and returned to more pressing matters. "I didn't have a chance to look round any further, because at that instant I heard the twins coming. If ever they find that head!—No! I'll not think on 't! They'll probably bowl it all over the lawn, or paint moustaches on it—I put nothing past them!"

"Let's hope they don't know you dropped it, and won't go looking for it."

"We can only hope." Then a new cloud smudged my fevered brow. "But what if one of your housemaids, more conscientious than the other, decides the hallway could use a good redding out, and suppose she starts poking round in all the nooks and crannies of the place, and suppose she comes across something she hadn't expected to find staring up at her? They'll hear her shrieks in the next county!"

Lady Eleanore rose and paced the floor nervously.

"Well, I wish I *could* take a look, because if that conscientious housemaid you mentioned—Bridget is her name—"

"The wall-eyed one with the horse face."

"That's right. If Bridget ever saw a thing like that—"

"Yes, but what do you mean, you *wish* you could take a look? Can't you go right now?"

She shook her head.

"Against the Code. No menial tasks allowed between the witching hour and cockcrow. No, Simon, I'm afraid that cold or no cold you'll have to get back down there before the housemaids show up and find that thing."

It wasn't fair. It wasn't fair at all, but that's the way things are in our business. She made me finish the soup and then left with a parting injunction.

"Don't be long now. Slip on some dry things and get going!"

nine

I T WAS ALL VERY WELL for someone who had not been through what I had been through to talk about getting going, but I was exhausted. The chicken soup had warmed and relaxed me, and bed had never felt better. Slowly, insidiously, the eyelids drooped.

When suddenly I started out of a sound sleep, the first grey light of day was visible through the curtains of my window. With a guilty cry I sprang out of bed, sneezed twice, and threw on some clothes. Mere moments later I was in the back hallway of the main house.

Breathing hard, I sent my glance darting round in hit-or-miss fashion. But then I got hold of myself. It was no time for panic. Almost inevitably my thoughts turned to one of my current heroes. What would Sherlock Holmes do?

I was a great admirer of Mr. Holmes, whose exploits I had followed in the newspapers. Within a few more years the whole world was to be grateful to Dr. Watson for providing his versions of the great detective's cases. It was not hard to imagine the cold, clear, logical, step-by-step process of deduction Holmes would bring to bear on such a problem as mine. What indeed would Sherlock Holmes do? Certainly, I told myself sharply, he would not run around like a chicken with its head cut off—an unfortunate simile I immediately banished from my mind with a curse. Sitting down on the bottom step, I folded my arms and gave myself up to Holmes-style concentration.

And, like the master, not without results.

In a short time, with a keen, almost ferretlike expression on my face, with my brows drawn into two hard black lines while my eyes shone out from beneath them with a steely glitter, I was carefully mounting the staircase.

I peeped round the corner into the corridor, still shadowy and dim in the early morning light. Sure enough, a thin ribbon of water stain preserved the path along which the head had rolled.

Next, starting at the top, and crouched down so that my nose almost touched the boards, I began to examine closely each tread of the staircase. The second tread rewarded my efforts.

My own wet footprint was still visible upon it, as well as the smaller ones of the twins, coming and going. Plainly, after finding no trace of me in the hallway, they had returned to bed. To one side of the surface of the tread, however, fortunately not obliterated by any of the footprints, was a small round wet spot.

"Ah-ha! What have we here?" I muttered to myself. Unquestionably it was the imprint made by the head on its first bounce.

I examined the next tread, and the next. Not until the fifth, however, did I find another round wet spot, slightly larger than the first.

I continued my search, and this time it was the ninth tread that exhibited a still larger round wet spot.

Bouncier and bouncier!

Hardly pausing in between, I moved on down five more steps, a sixth, and a seventh, and there, on the third step from the bottom, I found a still larger and rather splattery wet spot. Glancing ahead, I was able to discern the next round wet spot nearly dead center in the rectangular hallway.

Standing at the bottom of the stairs, I placed my finger on the third step and then traced an arc in the air to the spot on the floor, and from there a similar arc representing the probable trajectory of the next bounce.

Against the far wall, scarcely noticed till now, stood a great Chinese vase four feet tall. My tracing finger headed straight for it. I stared at the vase, then peered into its depths.

Reckless Rupert had scored two points!

I all but dove inside, but of course the wretched head was out of reach. After stretching my arms vainly, I concluded that the only possible solution was either to smash the vase or tip it over and roll the head out of it. Though I would have dearly loved to kick the Cantonese monstrosity to smithereens, I thought I could hear some of the staff stirring in the back regions of the house, and decided it would be more prudent to deny myself that satisfaction and tip it over instead.

Before I could touch the vase, however, certain all too familiar sounds sent me diving for cover instead. I had scarcely slipped behind a large tapestry of the Rape of the Sabines before the twins rounded the corner at the head of the stairs.

In a fierce whisper Johnny was saying, "You see? He left a trail of water right to these stairs, and then went down them, just like we thought."

"Well, come on, let's see where his trail goes."

They came slowly down the stairs, obviously examining them on the way.

"Those are his footprints."

"And here's ours."

"Look at this big round spot! Do you think he slipped and fell on his—"

"No, it's not big enough."

"You mean, his—"

"No! The spot!" said Ronny, and of course a lot of heartless giggling ensued.

"Here's another wet spot!" Johnny reported from the center of the hallway. "Hey, it's funny, too—this is the last one!"

"He must have taken a big jump from here and vanished somewhere."

"Yes, but where?"

"Well . . . Say!"

"What?"

"If he jumped from here he could have jumped into that big vase!"

"You're right! That's just the sort of thing he could vanish into, I'll bet! And if he did, it'll still be wet inside!"

I nearly let slip a churchyard groan. Rupert's head was a goner, and there was not one thing I could think of to do about it.

"Come on, let's look! Boost me up!"

"No, you boost me up!"

"I thought of it first!"

"You did not!"

"John! Ronald!" Like the voice of an angel from on high came the voice of their mother.

"Ma!" The twins groaned the homely appellation together. "Did those darn birds wake you up again?"

Her authoritative steps descended the stairs.

"What are you doing down here at this hour of the morning? I will not have you running around the halls disturbing your father and your brother and sister. How did the hall and the stairs get so wet?"

"Ma, it was the ghost!"

"The ghost? Have you boys been bothering the ghost again?"

"No, he was bothering us," said Johnny, "but we out-witted him."

"Again," said Ronny.

"I *knew* I heard some sort of disturbance during the night, and I tried to make your father go see what it was, but he said, 'Oh, it's only that pesky ghost again,' and went back to sleep. Well, we shall talk about this later—with your father. Right now I want you to get back to your room and stay there."

"Aw, but, Ma—"

"Now!" said Mrs. Otis, and she shooed them firmly ahead of her up the stairs. Blessing her, and blessing our boisterous British songbirds, I waited till footsteps and voices had died away in the upper hall. Then I sprang out from behind the tapestry and rushed to the vase, deter-mined not to lose another precious moment before someone else appeared.

Well, haste makes waste. In my haste, once again I for-got I was not firmed up to full strength and, like my armour, the ponderous vase got away from me. With a crash it toppled forward and smashed into a thousand pieces on the floor.

"Lord a' mercy, what was that?" cried a clacking female voice I knew at once to be Bridget's; and clomping foot-steps came swiftly my way from the nearest room. I was so

83

startled I never even thought of vanishing. Instead I snatched up Reckless Rupert's head from amongst the debris, tucked it under my arm, and returned to my hiding place seconds before Bridget barged in. She stopped short, and gasped.

"By all the saints, 'tis the Chinee vahse gone and got itself smashed! What will the marster say? Now, what could have made that great heathen pot go tumbling over?"

While Bridget was carrying on in this tiresome fashion, I was being threatened with a nasal disaster of cataclysmic proportions. I felt a sneeze coming on that would have torn the entire tapestry from the wall. Only by drawing upon my ultimate inner resources was I able to hold the sneeze at bay. Just when I felt I had subdued it, however—

"*Ah-h-h-h-C-H-O-O-O!*"

Under my arm, Reckless Rupert's head had sneezed.

I had forgot that it, too, had been drenched, and might have developed a head cold quite as heavy as my own. Not only did it sneeze, but it sneezed with such violence that the thrust of the sneeze caused the head to push aside the edge of the tapestry and protrude its gargoyle features into the open.

The grisly object might have escaped the notice of one of Bridget's out-turned eyes, but not both. She took half a look and let out a shriek which, as predicted earlier, was commented on seconds later in the next county. But at least she did not linger. Adding shriek upon shriek, she fled in the direction of the servants' hall, whilst I, regaining my wits at last, shifted gears sufficiently to vanish.

After an incident such as that, it seemed wise to lie low for a while, and certainly that was what I felt like doing. I took to my bed, eyes watering, nose running, wheezing and sneezing, and stayed there.

"With all the remedies there are in her confounded Red Cross kit, doesn't that Otis woman have something for a common cold?" I demanded irritably of my nurse during her next chicken soup run. "Have you really looked?"

"Yes. Doctor Dobell also puts out a cold pill."

"Never mind!"

"Anyway, nothing beats nature's remedy," said Lady Eleanore, and she shoved some more chicken soup into me.

"How did the household take Bridget's news?" I asked presently.

"About as you might expect. Everyone felt sure you were at the bottom of it, of course. The twins envied you greatly—they would have loved so to break a vase that size themselves. Mrs. Otis dosed Bridget with something called Simpson's Superior Soothing Syrup. Wash produced a bottle of Massingale's Miracle Mucilage and assured everyone he would have the vase glued back together in no time. The Minister wondered if he could collect insurance on it. Miss Virginia cried, because she had wanted to paint it and hadn't been able to."

Lady Eleanore's recital of their reactions fair took the heart out of me, what little I had left. I picked at the coverlet with disconsolate fingers.

"I give up on the lot of them," I said. "Honestly, I've just about had it—as that mysterious voice said to me so long ago. I wish . . ."

I paused, appalled at my own wish, but then blurted it out anyway.

"I wish I could get away from this place!"

It was the first time in three hundred years that such a

thought had crossed my mind, but now I knew it had been shaping up ever since the present Lord and Lady Canterville had deserted me, and before I even knew they had done so. For centuries I had been happy there at Canterville Chase, with my Reverend Dampiers and Lady Barbaras and Madame de Tremouillacs to keep me amused. But now, first the family stayed away, and then the Otises turned up. And these Americans had done what endless generations of the British nobility had been unable to do. They had taken the bloom off everything.

Lady Eleanore gazed at me in astonishment. The hand that held the spoon trembled so badly that drops of hot soup spilled on my bare chest.

"Ow! Watch what you're doing, Elly!"

"I'm sorry, but you startled me. Did I hear you rightly?"

I could not blame her for being astonished. At any earlier date I should have been astonished myself. But now . . .

"Look, Elly," I said, sitting up on one elbow, "the world is changing. Attitudes are changing. People—especially these benighted Yankees—are becoming intolerably pragmatic. After all, nothing stays in fashion forever. Maybe Stately Homes haunting is on its way out. I tell you, I'm beginning to feel housebound!"

"You mean, you'd really like to . . . to . . ."

"Well, isn't there something else I could do, something that would give me a chance to get away and travel? When you stop to think about it, Elly, I've never been anywhere except for that one little honeymoon jaunt of ours through France and Italy, and I hated France. All those Frenchmen. I was too late for the Crusades, and too early for the outposts of Empire. I've always wanted to see more of the world—I can't tell you how many times I've pored over Thomas Cook's brochures in the library—but instead here I am, mouldering away in a corner of Berkshire, vegetating in the provinces!"

Lady Eleanore gazed at me and through me with troubled eyes, lost in thought. She took a long time to mull it all over. When she had finished, she roused herself with a sigh.

"I'll look into it," she said, with curious sadness in her voice. "I can't promise anything, but I'll look into it."

The winds of change were blowing, to be sure—but as is so often the case, not from the expected quarter.

ten

MY DAYS WERE NOW an agony of suspenseful fidgeting as I waited for some word from Lady Eleanore as to my fate. Was there a chance of my escaping from Canterville Chase, or was I doomed to stay on forever? Now that I had finally faced my true feelings about the place, I longed for release like a soul in torment.

One morning, having pretty well recovered from my cold, I was standing at my window idly surveying the ancestral acres and wishing I had something to do, when I saw a messenger approaching on a bicycle. Thinning myself out, I slipped into the hallway and down the stairs, curious to know what the message might be. It was shameful to be reduced to such mere busybody activities, but I welcomed anything that might pass some time.

As I had expected at that hour, I found the Minister sitting alone in a black leather-covered armchair, growling over his morning newspaper. In a moment Shadwell, the butler, entered with stately tread and a silver salver upon which rested a yellow envelope.

"This has just arrived for you, sir."

"Thank you, Shadwell. If there is an answer to be sent, I'll call you."

Shadwell withdrew, and the Minister opened his telegram, obviously expecting nothing of any great importance. His eyes scanned the contents.

"Oh, God!" roared Minister Otis, and he fell back in his chair like a stricken man. His outcry was so desperate it brought Wash into the room on the run.

"Pa! Pa, what is the matter?"

The Minister pointed feebly to the telegram, which had fluttered to the floor from his nerveless fingers. Wash snatched it up and read it.

"No!" He staggered like a man who had taken a bullet, as once again the wire fluttered to the floor.

"What is it, Washington?" Drawn to the scene as well by her husband's distress signal, Mrs. Otis entered the room. Wash had moved to the mantelpiece and was clutching it for support. Noticing the telegram, his mother stooped with a graceful movement, picked it up, and read. With commendable forethought, Wash turned and hurried to her side, reaching her just in time.

"Oh!" moaned Mrs. Otis, and swooned into her son's arms.

He swept her up and deposited her gently on a sofa. He was kneeling beside her, patting her wrists and saying, "Mother! Mother, are you all right?" when Virginia came hurrying in. She helped Wash bring their mother around, all the while asking, "What happened? Wash, what is it?"

In answer he pointed silently. Once more the telegram was retrieved, read, dropped.

"Oh, *no!*" Virginia sat down with a thump and burst into a storm of tears.

By this time the Minister had recovered himself enough to struggle out of his chair and totter to his wife's side.

"Come, we must help your mother to her room. For

that matter, we will all need time to pull ourselves together. We are in no condition to discuss this matter now," he said grimly, as he and Wash raised Mrs. Otis to her feet. "In half an hour let us gather here again to decide what is to be done."

With Virginia following, still weeping stormily, they helped the half-conscious woman from the room.

I had never been more surprised. I had thought nothing in the world or out of it could upset that family. What crushing blow had fallen on the House of Otis to provoke a response such as this? Had they lost all their money? Had the American Minister been summoned home to Washington in disgrace? I wasted no time in having a look at the fatal message. It was brief:

ARRIVE ASCOT 5:36 PM STOP SEND CARRIAGE STOP
HENRY BENTON

Henry Benton? Who was Henry Benton, and why should the simple news of his impending arrival throw the Otis family into such a state of shock? Before I had time to do more than scan the message, however, I heard the great front door open with a bang, and the sound of familiar footsteps. I barely had time to withdraw to a corner of the room before they rushed in merry as grigs. I had let go of the message so convulsively that it was still in the midst of its fifth flutter to the floor when they arrived.

"Coo! What's that blowing around?"

"Looks like a telegram! Let's have a look!"

Johnny pounced on it, and they both struggled to hold it.

"Come on, let me read it!"

"Stop pulling, now *I* can't read it. . . ."

But then they both did read it, and this time the wire

fluttered to the floor from four hands. They stared at each other.

"I think I'm going to be sick," said Ronny.

"So am I," said Johnny, and they made an urgent exit toward the great outdoors.

Now I was *really* impressed. I went to my perch on the bookcase and settled down to wait.

When the elder Otises reassembled, the wisdom of the recess ordered by the Minister was evident. Mrs. Otis was pale but composed. Virginia had subdued her tears. Wash and his father had command of themselves. Faces were long, but at least under control.

The Minister made the opening address.

"Maybe we should all pack up and get out of here while we can," he said, but this suggestion was immediately cried down.

"I *can't* leave here now!" said Virginia passionately. "I *won't!*"

"Nor I!" blurted Wash. Then he grew self-conscious under his father's sharp glance and added lamely, "I—I like it here."

"I will not be driven from my own home," said Mrs. Otis, and she looked as annoyed as I had ever seen her. "Really, it's not fair! Everyone thought your Cousin Henry was safely settled in Haiti, pursuing his study of that wretched voodooism he became so interested in. What ever made him come to England now—of all times, now?"

"What do you think?" snorted the Minister. "Somehow he heard I had bought this place. And one thing we do know, once he sees this house with all its creature comforts, we won't get him out of it for months and months! Henry

Benton is a professional houseguest, he's spent *years* of his life in other people's homes, including ours, and he's the very worst of the lot," said Minister Otis, warming to his subject. "Even though he's my own flesh and blood, I'll say it—he's the most obnoxious person I've ever known. Once he gets his foot in the door, he's impossible to get rid of until he's good and ready to go, as we all know. Nothing fazes him—hints, insults, even threats—and you know we can't go too far in that line, anyway, as long as the matter of Aunt Julia's trust fund remains unsettled. He could be very troublesome in that area if he became provoked enough to make the effort. No, he has us at his mercy. Unless we flee at once and go live in some Welsh village under assumed names, I don't see what we can do but bite the bullet."

Virginia burst out again.

"But we *can't* have him here! We *can't!*" she stormed. Then she took a deep breath and began to choose her words more carefully. "Mama has invited the duke of Cheshire down for a visit. Now, I know I'm too young to think of marriage, and I'm not in love with him or anything like that at all, but still, supposing—just *supposing*—that someday I *might* fall in love with him and he might fall in love with me and we might decide to marry. . . ."

Virginia's mother, I noted, was listening to these suppositions without the slightest appearance of disapproval. It would have been a strange American mother of that day and age who would have opposed a possible connection with one of Britain's oldest, noblest, and wealthiest families.

"I'm not saying we will, just that someday we *might*," continued Virginia. "But if Cousin Henry is here when Cecil visits us, that day will never come, because Cousin Henry will butt into everything, and—and make his terrible jokes, and—because nobody in his right mind would marry a girl if he knew Cousin Henry was part of her family!" she concluded, and burst into tears again.

"Hear, hear," said Wash in a low voice.

A gloom that was almost palpable settled over the gathering.

"I can see him now, swilling down my best wine, taking a fistful of my best cigars—'One for now and a couple for later with a glass in my room before bedtime,'" mused the Minister, mimicking a voice even more rasping than his own, if he was doing it justice.

"*I* can hear him making remarks about my personal appearance, as though I were still ten years old," groaned Wash. "And he'll probably still call me Washy."

"I don't even want to *think* about what he'll say to me," declared Virginia with a shudder.

"What about you, Lucretia?"

Mrs. Otis raised a beautiful, tragic face. It reminded one of the face of Mary, Queen of Scots, on her way to the scaffold.

"There are not many things in this life I cannot stand, Hiram," she said, "but one of them is your Cousin Henry."

The American Minister bowed his head.

"I have always been grateful to you for marrying me in spite of him," he said. "His conduct at our wedding . . . well, there is no point in raking up painful memories. . . ."

And then they all began to say over again most of the things they had already said, as people always do when they find themselves faced with an impossible situation, but I was no longer listening. My mind was otherwise occupied, seething with possibilities, churning with half-formulated plans that rapidly took shape. The Otises were all so wrapped up in their own unhappy thoughts and their fruitless discussion that none of them noticed the shape which was firming up in a corner of the library. Not until I stepped forward did they glance around; not till then did four pairs of eyes grow suddenly round.

"Good morning," I said in an icy tone of voice. "I have a proposition to advance."

In this instance I was not in costume, of course, but was wearing the ordinary ruff, doublet, and hose of an Elizabethan gentleman. There was nothing of the grisly, the nauseous, or the gruesome about my appearance, yet it drew a considerably more gratifying response than had been the case on past occasions. All four Otises started up out of their chairs and gaped at me. Their despair had obviously lowered their resistance to shocks.

"Bless my soul, it's the ghost!" cried the Minister.

"Good heavens!" said Mrs. Otis. "I must confess, sir, you startled me."

It was Virginia who recovered the most quickly.

"Sir Simon, have you been listening to our conversation?"

"I have. That is why I decided to reveal myself, under a flag of truce, so to speak. You shall put the matter of your Cousin Henry in my hands, in return for which you shall agree never again to meddle in my affairs in any way, but allow me to discharge my duties in this house unmolested."

I'll say one thing for Yankees, they are quick to sense a good bargain. Rapid glances flashed among them, a wild hope kindled in all eyes, and Minister Otis turned to me with a bow that was almost obsequious.

"Take a chair, sir, please do!"

"I prefer to stand," I replied severely, and folded my arms on my chest. "Pray be seated, all of you."

"As you wish, sir," said the Minister, popping into a

chair. He gazed at me wonderingly. "By George! You know, the way you look right now you could almost be a normal human being, if it weren't for those funny clothes."

"*Funny?*"

"Oh, I don't mean *funny*, I just mean—well, different. Do I take it you have a plan for ridding us of our unwanted guest?"

"I do. And do you accept my terms?"

"Oh, yes!"

"All of you?"

Three eager voices joined the Minister's in assent.

"But can you speak for the twins as well?"

"Oh, you bet we can! Why, if you can handle Cousin Henry, you'll be their hero for life. He is the only person in the world who has ever consistently made *their* lives miserable!"

"We are agreed, then. Now, as to your cousin. From a remark Mrs. Otis made earlier, I gather that his avocation has been the study of the voodoo religion in Haiti."

The Minister nodded.

"Up to his ears!"

"His ears do not matter. It is his Achilles' heel we are interested in, and I think we may have found it. He arrives on the 5:36 train this evening at Ascot, I believe. In that case, we haven't much time, and everyone will have to help."

"Just say the word!"

"We shall leave nothing to chance. We shall build this evening into a full production such as only I, Sir Simon de Canterville, can create. Each of you will be players in it, and I expect nothing less than peak performances from all concerned."

For the first time, the Minister looked uncertain.

"You may count on all of us, I'm sure," he said, glancing at the others, "but it's a lot to ask of the twins."

"It is indeed," I agreed, "and for that reason the parlour-maids Sheila and Bridget will take them to the seashore for a brief holiday. The twins will like that, and it will do Bridget's nerves a world of good. I would suggest Brighton. In fact, we shall immediately send all the servants on holiday except Mrs. Umney."

"Mrs. Umney? But will she—?"

"Leave Mrs. Umney to me. She has more courage and resources than you might think, and we shall need her. And now our preparations must begin, for there is not a moment to lose. Washington, the first task is yours."

"Yes, sir!"

"Go fetch that foul detergent stick of yours and get to work on the great front door," I told him. "I want every trace of oil removed from its hinges!"

eleven

A T HALF-PAST SIX that evening, under lowering skies, a waggonette with one new wheel drew up before Canterville Chase and a large, fleshy gentleman stepped down. He wore muttonchop whiskers and his grey hair parted in the middle. The driver's helper hurried up the broad stone steps with a travelling bag, all but flung it down beside the entrance, and rushed back to the vehicle. With scarcely a civil word of farewell, the driver whipped up his team and sent the carriage hurtling away down the drive.

The portly gentleman snorted scornfully, shook his head, and then turned away with a shrug. Sweeping his small, greedy eyes from side to side along the stately facade that confronted him, he began to smile, as though in anticipation of many good things. Mounting the steps to the entrance, he gave the bellpull a tug. There was a pause, and then dragging footsteps could be heard inside. A rattle of chains, and the great door slowly creaked open. A crone of hideous aspect peered out at him from a dim interior. It was all he could do to repress a start at the sight of her.

"Good evening, sir. You'd be Mr. Benton, I'll warrant. I bid you welcome to Canterville Chase," she croaked in a sombre voice, and bowed him inside.

97

At that moment Minister Otis hurried out into the entrance hall with hands outstretched.

"Henry! At last you're here! I can't tell you what the sight of a familiar face means to us just now!"

Cousin Henry had a confused look about him as his hand was pumped. No doubt he was unprepared for so warm a welcome, being long hardened to less effusive greetings.

"What do you mean, Hiram?" he asked.

"Never mind, Henry, time enough later to explain . . . everything. Where is your luggage?"

"I have a bag outside. The rest of my things will be sent along tomorrow. I came straight from the boat. Those fellers you sent for me, by the way—didn't think much of 'em. All but threw my bag out when we got here. Never saw such a nervous pair."

"Yes, yes, well, I'm afraid that— But never mind, let's not mar this happy moment with— Mrs. Umney will bring in your bag."

"Yes, sir." Mrs. Umney shuffled outside. Along with a number of other unattractive physical features, she seemed to carry one shoulder higher than the other.

"Hiram, what on earth are you doing having a creature like that answer your door?" Cousin Henry demanded in a gruff voice almost before she had gone. "Where's your butler?"

"I'm afraid we have a servant problem. But never mind that now, come in, come in!" said the Minister, urging his cousin toward the library. "Everybody's waiting!"

In the library the newcomer again found himself being greeted with a kind of nervous warmth that surprised him. He responded with his customary brand of joviality.

"Well, Lucretia!" he said, giving her two hearty smacks,

one on the lips, "still the best-looking gal that ever came out of West Fifty-third Street! And look at little Ginny! Not exactly a child any more, budding out a bit here and there, eh?—heh-heh! Washy, my boy! You've gotten tall, and you'd be a lot taller if there wasn't so much turned under for feet, he-he! What's this you're offering me, a hand or a ham?"

Through all of this four Spartan smiles remained steady. Desperation can make actors out of almost anyone.

"It's good to see you, Henry," said Mrs. Otis in a deep and troubled voice that almost broke as she added, "We do so need . . . company. . . ."

"You do? Why?"

"Now, now, Lucretia! Never mind," interrupted Minister Otis, moving to the refreshment table. "Time enough to go into that later. Henry, I expect you'd like a sip of something. There's a lot of excellent sherry in the cellars of this house, and I've decanted a bottle of the best to welcome you with. I've also had a bottle put in your room, knowing how much you enjoy a glass before bedtime."

"Well, now!" marvelled Cousin Henry, who usually had to demand such attentions. "Pour away, Hiram, I'm parched!"

When glasses had been filled, with even a thimbleful for Virginia—"A special treat for a special occasion!" said her father—the Minister raised his glass.

"Welcome to Canterville Chase, Henry!"

Cousin Henry was the type who could be counted on to drink promptly, and he did so now.

"Faugh!"

With a strangled expression he turned and spat into the fireplace.

99

"Vinegar!"

The Minister sipped, and set his glass aside with a grimace.

"Good grief, you're right—it's gone bad! And yet I decanted the bottle myself, and tasted it, and it was all right not an hour ago!"

Mrs. Otis sank against the cushions, the back of one pale hand against her brow.

"Are we to be spared nothing?" she murmured brokenly.

"Is this the twins' work?" barked Cousin Henry.

"No, they're not here. They've been sent off for safekeeping to the seashore."

"They've been—*what?* The twins? How could they ever need safekeeping?"

The sound of horses' hooves and the rattle of wheels outside caused Minister Otis to hold up his hand for silence. Washington stepped to a window.

"Is that the carriage, Washington?"

"Yes, Father."

"Good."

Cousin Henry was looking from one face to another with growing concern.

"Hiram, what the devil is going on around here?"

The Minister glanced at his family, then dropped his shoulders with a sigh.

"I was hoping we could have a few happy moments together before—before— But I see it's not to be. Henry, we are in a difficult situation here, and your arrival is most providential. We are hoping that you, with your knowledge of the occult, through your studies of voodooism, may be able to help us. Henry, this house is said to be haunted. And of course, these ridiculous Englishmen take such things seriously. Lord Canterville himself warned me against the ghost. It's embarrassing even to mention such nonsense in this day and age, but there you are. And to be sure, annoyances have been occurring with enough regularity to make us feel persecuted."

Cousin Henry greeted the news with the keen, clinical— and skeptical—look of an expert. On the whole, he looked pleased.

"Well! We'll find out about that soon enough. A few simple experiments . . . But are you sure this is not all an attempt by purely mortal hands to drive you away from this house?" he asked, casting a spiteful glance at Mrs. Umney, who, summoned by her mistress, had shuffled in to collect the sherry glasses. "What do you know about this alleged ghost?"

The minister pointed to the floor in front of the fireplace, where a dull red stain glowed malevolently.

"On that very spot, in 1575, the fourth earl, Sir Simon de Canterville, murdered his wife, Lady Eleanore. Ever since that day the bloodstain has remained there, and nothing can eradicate it."

Cousin Henry peered down at the stain.

"Have you ever tried Pinkerton's?" he asked. "Somebody sent me a stick of it, and—"

"We have tried everything," interrupted Wash, "and nothing touches it."

"Hmm. Well, then, let it alone. It's probably a flaw in the wood. Are you telling me, then, that this Sir Simon feller is supposed to be the ghost?"

"Yes."

"Just because he murdered his wife? Haw! From what I've seen of women—most women, that is, present company excepted, heh-heh—she probably deserved it."

Mrs. Umney's head came up.

"Not her!" she cried. "She was a saint, was Lady Eleanore, a perfect saint!"

"That will do, Mrs. Umney," said Mrs. Otis, but the old housekeeper continued to grumble as she shuffled out.

"Do you have to put up with much of that?" Cousin Henry asked in biting tones.

"She is the only servant we have been able to keep," said Mrs. Otis. "All the others have fled."

"Fled?"

"Fled."

"Why?"

Minister Otis pointed a finger toward the window.

"Let me tell you why that carriage is waiting out in the drive, Henry. Every evening, as soon as it grows dark, the carriage is brought round, and it stays there till the first light of day—because there is one eventuality of which we live in constant dread!"

A croaking voice spoke from the doorway.

"Dinner is served, ma'am."

Mrs. Otis shuddered.

"Oh, dear," she said. "Well, we may as well go in."

"But wait a minute!" cried Cousin Henry. "What about—"

"Never mind," said the Minister, forcing a cheery note back into his voice. "Time enough for that later. We're perfectly safe as long as we're all together. Will you take Lucretia in?"

Cousin Henry hesitated.

"Oh, very well," he said crossly. "I must say, after the trip here, I am famished!"

"I'm glad to hear that," replied the Minister, "because around here you'll have to be."

Dinner consisted of an indescribable soup followed by an incredible main course.

"Good Lord!" groaned the Minister. "Not charred lamb shanks again!"

"Please, Hiram!" said Mrs. Otis. "She'll hear."

Cousin Henry stared at them incredulously.

"Do you mean to tell me that old witch does the cooking, too?" He was appalled. Being one of those persons who can eat anything while complaining about everything, however, he managed to find a few bits of meat that had escaped the worst of the flames. At the same time, his jowly countenance made it abundantly clear he found the meal far from satisfactory. And meanwhile, of course, his curiosity had not abated. The Otises strove nobly to restrict the conversation to family gossip, but in time his patience gave out.

"Hiram, I wish you'd stop beating around the bush," he said. "Just what is going on around here? What's the carriage out there for? What is that 'one eventuality' you say you're in such dread of?"

Minister Otis sighed again, heavily.

"I had hoped we could have a happy little dinner together, without having to spoil it, before—"

"Don't worry about spoiling *this* dinner!" snapped Cousin Henry. "What is it that has made you so jumpy?"

"Very well, you shall have it. It is the fear that one of us will see the ghost."

"Ah! You mean, you really do believe in him, then!"

"No, Henry, I do not believe in ghosts—but in this instance I should hate to find I was wrong! So I am taking no chances. Let me explain. Let me give you the history of the Canterville Ghost."

"Let's hear it."

"Well, his reported appearances are extremely rare but, with a single exception, they would seem to have been fatal. In 1596 the family chaplain was the first person to alarm the household with an hysterical report of having seen the ghost. Exactly twenty-four hours later the poor man started up from a chair and fell dead. In this very room. And that part of the story, at least, has been authenticated. The ghost was next seen in 1692 by a visiting Scottish earl. The earl, who was a superstitious man and who had heard the legend of the family chaplain, left at once on horseback, intending to put as much distance as he could between himself and Canterville Chase. Exactly twenty-four hours later he was thrown from his fourth mount as though some terrible force had hurled him off, and his neck was broken. Then in 1788 the ghost was reported by the daughter of a visiting family. Luckily for her, however, the fourteenth earl of Canterville had made quite a study of such matters, and had read that ghosts could not pursue their victims across open water. The young lady was rushed to Brighton and put aboard a vessel which, after a perilous voyage, finally made its way to France. She lived on the Continent to a ripe old age, but never risked a return to England."

The minister allowed himself a dramatic pause, then concluded his explanation.

"That is why the carriage always stands ready after dark. As I said, I don't believe in ghosts, but I intend to take no chances. Should Lucretia or either of the children or I actually see the Canterville Ghost, he or she will be taken at once to Dover by the quickest way and put aboard the first boat across the Channel."

The minister spread his hands wide in an appeal to judgment.

"Am I being a credulous fool, Henry?"

With his elbows on the arms of his chair, the expert placed his fingertips together and considered.

"No, hardly that," he declared. "I've run across too many cases in my studies—cases remarkably similar in some respects. . . . You've noticed, I suppose, that the ghost's victims have always been outsiders, never members of the Canterville family?"

"That struck you, too, did it?"

"Of course. And it's an important point. There may be real danger here, I assure you! In any event, why do you take unnecessary risks? Why do you stay here? Why put up with all this? Why don't you get out of this house and—"

"What? Why, if word ever got back to Washington that I'd let myself be run out of my house by a ghost, my political enemies would ruin me with the story! My career would be finished," cried Minister Otis. "Besides, the ghost's appearances have been rare—every ninety-six years, as you may have noticed. Of course, that part is awkward, since, unfortunately, this is the ninety-sixth year since his last reported appearance. Nevertheless, we are determined to see it through. The family is sticking by me. If we can just last it out till the end of the year, we should be safe."

Cousin Henry was outraged.

"See it through? What kind of madness is this? How can you even consider exposing your family to such dangers, merely for the sake of your blasted political career? Believe me, I know something about these matters, and— Hiram, you must give up this house and find another! We shall start looking for a suitable one tomorrow!"

The minister appeared shaken by Cousin Henry's vehemence.

"You really feel . . . ?"

"I do! I'd even be willing to stay with you for a few months and help you get settled."

"Well . . . I shall certainly give your suggestion some thoughtful consideration."

"Consideration my foot! I won't hear of anything else!"

"Well . . . Henry, I must say I feel better," said Minister Otis, brightening. "If there *is* such a creature as the Canterville Ghost, the feller knows by now he has a formidable adversary on the scene—"

"Don't talk of adversaries," said Cousin Henry sharply, almost nervously. "My only aim is to get you away from here."

"I was only joking," said the minister. "Come, let's leave the table with the ladies and have our cigars and port in the library."

"Very well, but I hope the port is better than the sherry," grumbled Cousin Henry as they rose.

In the library Minister Otis poured two glasses of ruby red port, sipped one, and looked relieved.

"I think you'll find this more to your taste."

Cousin Henry sniffed suspiciously, and took a cautious sip. Then he too smiled.

"Now, that's more like it! I'll take that decanter with me to my room when I go up—only way to be sure!"

"Please do! And try one of these with your wine," said the Minister, opening a large box of cigars.

"One for now, and a couple for later, heh-heh," said Cousin Henry, taking four and putting three in his pocket. Biting off an end, he held his cigar to the flame Minister Otis offered. Sitting back, he puffed out a thick cloud of smoke.

"Excellent, excellent. You always did have good taste in cigars, Hiram."

Bang!

Cousin Henry stared cross-eyed at the shredded cigar in his mouth.

"Good Lord! That was meant for me!" cried the Minister. He stared at the cigar he had been on the point of lighting, and hurled it into the fireplace.

Bang!

Cousin Henry slammed the remains of his cigar into the fireplace.

"This is the work of a demon! Hiram, we cannot put up with this any longer! We must find another house tomorrow!"

"You've convinced me," said the Minister sadly. "So be it! . . . Well, I know this has been very upsetting to all of us, and you must be tired after your journey. We'll have a busy day of it tomorrow, too, so we'd best get some rest. I'll see you to your room, if you'd care to call it a night."

"Well . . . yes, I think I *will* retire," said Cousin Henry with some hesitation, and not neglecting to possess himself of the decanter of port as he passed the table. When good-nights had been said, the Minister lighted two bedroom candles, gave one to Cousin Henry, and led him out.

The weather had undergone a nice change for the worse since the guest's arrival. Wind whistled round the house, rattling every door and window. Owls brushed the windows with silent wings, tapping on the panes with their cruel beaks to attract attention. From the old yew tree in the family burial ground, ravens croaked their tales of madness and death, while in the distance dogs howled like wolves. The flames of the candles the men carried flickered uneasily, throwing grotesque shadows on the walls as they mounted the stairs. Cousin Henry could be observed to lick his lips, and only when the Minister had ushered him into a sumptuous bedroom did he regain something of his normal attitude.

"Well, I must say this is quite handsome, Hiram. Too bad I'll have to give it up so soon," he said regretfully. "But never mind, we'll find something equally as good." He glanced around, and added with a frown, "My bag does not seem to have been brought up."

"Oh, dear, I'm sorry, Mrs. Umney should have attended to it."

"I won't be sorry to see the last of *her*. I'll help Lucretia line up a decent staff of servants at the new place, so that we can at least be comfortable, and properly fed."

"I'm sure she'll welcome your help, Henry. Sleep well, and thank you for coming to rescue us!"

"Little did I know, or I'd have been here sooner!"

"I'll send Washington up at once with your bag."

"Do."

When the Minister had gone, Cousin Henry poured himself a glass of port and sat down. Then his hand went to his pocket as he remembered the cigars he was carrying. He took them out and looked at them angrily.

"Damn! What a waste!"

He rose and started across the room, perhaps with the idea of opening the French windows to throw them out. Before he had taken two steps, however, a great gust of wind suddenly smashed the windows open, and a flash of lightning lividly illuminated something standing on the balcony.

Its broad shoulders supported a neck, but there was no head upon the neck. Instead, there was a terrible object tucked underneath one arm, whilst the other arm came up to point with chilling certainty at the trembling wretch in the bedroom. . . .

Minister Otis and his son happened to be standing at the foot of the stairs, Wash with the traveling bag in his hand, when Cousin Henry came down them three at a time.

"Henry!" cried the Minister. "What's the matter?"

"I–I–I–"

"Henry! You didn't—"

"I–I–"

"You saw the—"

"Yes!"

"Heaven protect us!" The Minister staggered, but recovered himself quickly. He seized his cousin's arm. "Come. You can depend on the coachman. He knows what to do."

When their guest had scrambled into the landau and Wash had thrown his bag in after him, Minister Otis took his hand.

"We'll send your luggage along as soon as you let us know where you are. We won't rest till we hear!" he said, but Cousin Henry was not even listening.

"Driver!" he cried, and away they went.

I waited till I heard the carriage leave. Then I walked into the corridor to the top of the staircase. Below me, in the entrance hall, the four Otises had gathered, and had collapsed into side chairs that stood at intervals along the walls. They looked up at me, and then as one the Otises came to their feet to give me a standing ovation. What could I do but take a bow? Having done so, I turned away and vanished, but when I regained the Tapestry Chamber their applause was still ringing in my ears.

twelve

ONE MIGHT THINK after a triumph of such magnitude I would have once again been my old sunny self, happy with my lot. And for a day or two I was.

"Simon, your ears should be burning. You're the hero of the hour," Lady Eleanore reported. "And they're still amazed at the way Mrs. Umney rallied round to do her bit. 'I think it was most courageous of you, Mrs. Umney,' the mistress said to me, and I said, 'Well, ma'am, I *am* used to Sir Simon by now, and once you get used to him he's not so bad.' All the same I've been given a nice rise in salary."

"And I a rise in their estimation."

"Yes, indeed. You'll have no more trouble from the Otis family."

"Not even from the twins?"

"They have solemnly promised to turn over a new leaf. Of course, they weren't told everything, but they know you were responsible for getting rid of Cousin Henry. Wash even had his joke about that—'We all helped,' he said, 'but Sir Simon was the moving spirit.' Oh, and another thing—it has been agreed that the bloodstain is never to be touched again."

That conversation, as much as anything, brought on a

period of moody introspection that came to a head a few nights later.

"Well," said Lady Eleanore one evening when she came by for our nightly chat, a habit we had gradually developed, "the great day has finally come."

"What?" I sprang up excitedly. "You mean, you have good news for me?"

She gave me a shocked look.

"Simon! Are you still thinking about leaving?"

"Of course!"

"But I thought, now that you're the cock of the walk around here, you'd be only too happy to settle down again."

"Settle down! That's it to a tee, and that's what's wrong. At first I couldn't understand why, day by day, I began to feel more discontented than ever, but now I do. Don't you see? What future is there for me here now? To plod through my Saturday and odd-Wednesdays commitments like a postman on his rounds, unmolested—and unmolesting! To find myself a sort of family pet of these people, spoken of with affection like an old family retainer—what sort of existence is that likely to be, other than one of utter boredom? No, it won't do. It won't do, Elly. I've got to get away, and you've got to help me."

"I see." She looked dreadfully disappointed, but she did not try to argue with me. She simply said, "Well, nothing has come through as yet, but I'll keep trying."

"I can't ask for more than that," I admitted.

The tone of our conversation had become depressing, so I steered it back to her opening remark.

"But tell me, what *did* you mean when you said the great day has finally come?"

She cheered up a bit, and smiled.

"The young duke of Cheshire has finally arrived to spend

the last week of his holidays here before he has to return to Eton."

"Young Cecil? Well, well! From what I've heard of him, I'm sure I'll like the lad. He's got good stuff in him, including Canterville blood."

"He has? I didn't know that."

"Oh, certainly you did. You've simply forgotten. Remember that first cousin of mine, the one we called Piggy?"

"Oh, yes," said Lady Eleanore. "Her. Why, of course—I remember now! She married the sixth duke of Cheshire, the one we called Blister." Her glance slyly teased me. "How nice! Here's a chance for the Cantervilles to be connected with the Otises."

"Heaven forfend! I'll admit that as a sort of Canterville Chase Repertory Company on Cousin Henry's Night, they pleased me well enough, but that does not mean their old deficiencies are all forgiven and forgotten. Still and all, I confess I am rather fond of Miss Virginia. It would do my heart good to see her married—*anything* to get her away from that family of hers!"

"Married? Now? But Simon, she's only fifteen."

"Juliet was fourteen."

"Yes, and look how her marriage turned out. Besides, Cecil could not possibly marry until he is of age. Those guardians of his can see to that. However, there is nothing to prevent their becoming engaged—a three-year engagement would be just right—and I'm sure that if the weather stays fair, so that they can ride through the park and stroll through the shrubbery a few times, Virginia will be showing off a solitaire within four-and-twenty hours. And the weather *will* stay fair," Lady Eleanore added with quiet authority.

"You women! There's nothing you like better than matchmaking."

"Maybe so, but in this case there is just enough spice in it to make it a challenge. I've already had a nice chat with Cecil's valet over a cup of tea, and he told me all about the row Cecil had with his guardians about his coming here at all. They did everything they could to stop him, especially his senior guardian, old Lord Grubb. Don't forget how they acted that first time, when he proposed on the spot. Packed him off back to Eton, they did."

I nodded. "In tears, I believe you said? Seemed rather unmanly, but then we Englishmen spend most of our time trying to hide how sentimental we really are. Perhaps the boy was sensible in letting it all out—and perhaps he may also have been making a foolhardy attempt to impress his guardians as to how seriously he meant his proposal."

"Now you're getting closer to the mark, I think, and foolhardy it was," said Lady Eleanore. "They *were* impressed, and as a result they've kept a close watch on him ever since."

I nodded darkly.

"No doubt old Grubb has ambitious plans for him, and no intention of allowing him to become involved with the daughter of an American commoner, however exalted his temporary rank."

"Exactly. So I'm sure the old schemer is at his wit's ends right now—but don't count him out. He's a sly old fox, is Lord Grubb."

"Love conquers all, even Grubbs," I said optimistically.

The next afternoon Lady Eleanore was back again, glowing with vicarious romance.

"Oh, Simon, you must come out! It's a joy to see those two romping together!"

"Well-a-day! And just how much romping are they doing?"

"Here, now, we'll have no coarse talk about our young lady, she's a good girl. I'm merely talking about fine animal spirits. But Simon, it's a lovely day, so why don't you go out and sit in the graveyard for a while, and perhaps you'll have a chance to see them."

It was true that ever since my triumphant comeback as Reckless Rupert I had scarcely been out of doors. A breath of fresh air was in order. So I took her suggestion, and was presently seated in comfortable invisibility on a gravestone, enjoying the afternoon sunshine as it filtered through me.

The tranquil scene was suddenly spoiled, however, by the intrusion of a small, wizened man wearing a bowler hat and a dreary black suit. Moving through the shrubbery in a sly and furtive manner, he abruptly sought conceal-ment behind an ancient oak tree not fifteen paces from where I sat. His reason for taking cover was quickly ap-parent as the twins came padding along from the opposite direction like two young hounds on a scent. Pulling to a halt in front of me, Johnny looked this way and that, stared through me, and said,

"Which way did they go?"

"Search me," said Ronny. The bowler hat peeped at them briefly, and I longed to cry "One of them is right behind you!" but that would have been unthinkable. Proper ghosts do not appear in broad daylight; it simply isn't done. But who was this trespasser, and how had the twins gotten onto his trail? Furthermore, Johnny's plural pronoun indi-cated that the man must have one or more confederates. When Johnny spoke again, however, I realized the lad was talking about our young lovers, and was unaware of the lurking intruder.

"Well, if you ask me," said Johnny, "it's a rotten trick playing hide-and-seek and not letting us play too!"

"Aw, she's sweet on him, that's why!"

Johnny sighed heavily.

"I know. Well, it had to happen sooner or later. Come on, let's keep looking for them."

"Which way?"

"This way," said Johnny, and they took up the chase in what turned out to be the wrong direction, because a moment later who should come racing along, from a different quarter, flushed and merry, but Miss Virginia. The bowler again peeped briefly. Running with the light-footed grace of Diana herself, Virginia sped past the graveyard and disappeared into a nearby copse.

Another moment, and here came Cecil, moving less quickly as he peered this way and that. He was soon eyeing the copse in a speculative manner, but before he could set off in that direction, the small man in the bowler appeared in plain view and stepped into his path. Cecil started violently, and drew back as from some venomous little adder.

"Mudge! What are you doing here?"

The small man removed his hat with greasy obsequiousness.

"Good afternoon, m' lord. His lordship sent me down with a communication of particular importance to you, sir," he said, and produced from an inner pocket a large legal document. "If you will be so good as to run your eye over it—the pertinent passages are marked—perhaps I shall be able to carry back to his lordship your acknowledgment that the matter is thoroughly understood. . . ."

Though he continued to regard Mudge with cold abhorrence, Cecil had turned pale. He was far too young to hide the flustered concern that had possessed him. With anxious eyes he perused the document and, as he did so, grew even paler. Mudge concealed—from Cecil, though not from me—a nasty little smirk behind the rim of his bowler.

"Well, m' lord?"

With an oath he must have learned during off hours at Eton, Cecil dashed the document to the ground.

"Damn you, Mudge, and damn him as well!" he cried with a fine show of spirit, but looking beaten all the same. This time Mudge hid his smirk with a low bow.

"Very good, m' lord. I shall pass along your message. And now I bid you a very good day."

Mudge lifted his bowler once again, replaced it on his head, and was gone, sliding away like a small serpent, whilst the young duke of Cheshire stood slumped in despair, glaring down bitterly at the papers on the ground. I expected more floods of tears; indeed, I hoped he would rush away weeping, because I was itching to get my hands on that document and learn what horrid consequence had overtaken the poor lad. But instead, his features hardened and set in a manly cast, and he retrieved the offending papers, hiding them carefully away inside his handsomely tailored linen jacket. Then, bracing himself, squaring his shoulders like a true Briton, he turned and took up the scent, the delicious scent of Miss Virginia. Gone, however, was the eager step, the sparkling glance, and gone the smile from his lips.

"I wonder what the little toad handed him?"

"A shock, that's for sure," said Lady Eleanore.

That evening I had hardly been able to wait till she turned up, and barely let her sit down in the second-best

chair before pouring out my tale of Cecil's woe. She found
my story doubly interesting, since it explained something
that had been troubling her ever since our young lovers had
returned to the house from their afternoon romp.

"I was that worried, when I saw them," she declared,
resorting to an Umneyism. "You never saw a more woebegone pair in your life. Formal, silent, walking about six feet
apart. Biting their lips, avoiding each other's eyes. I thought
they had merely had some silly quarrel, but now I can see
it's more than that."

"Of course it is. The young duke has some dreadful
secret. He has become distant and reserved. Virginia is upset and baffled and dying of curiosity, and so am I. Elly, we
must have a look at that document. Old Grubb is behind it,
of course, I'm sure of that—but what is it he's come up
with?"

"Well, there's only one way to find out, Simon, and right
now is an ideal time to do so. The young people cast such a
pall over everything—Wash isn't looking any too well,
either—that everyone went to bed early except for Cecil,
and he's put on a dismal hat and a gloomy Inverness cape
and gone out to stride across the moors."

"Moors? We don't have any moors around here."

"Don't worry, his frame of mind will make our meadows
as bleak as moors. So nip over and have a look in the Royal
Bedchamber."

"Is that where he's been installed? Lah-de-dah!"

"Well, of course. Rank has its privileges."

"Why don't you go have a look, Elly?"

"Me? Why, it would be worth my place if Mrs. Umney
was ever caught snooping around in a guest's bedroom at
this time of night! Anyway, why do you hesitate, Simon?
It's a job that's right up your alley."

"Listen, I still don't trust those twins! Are you sure it's safe?"

"Of course it's safe. Go find that document and have a look at it. I'll wait here till you return."

Travelling through back corridors, I made my way to the Royal Bedchamber. The house was indeed quiet. A low drone from the master bedroom indicated that the Minister was peacefully sawing wood. I thought I heard the sound of muffled weeping coming from behind Miss Virginia's door, but couldn't be sure. Not a sound was to be heard from the Royal Bedchamber. When I got up my nerve to try the door and enter, I found the room to be as Lady Eleanore had predicted, unoccupied.

My search did not take long. I simply cast my mind back to the days when I was a young nitwit of Cecil's age and asked myself where I would have secreted important papers. Then I moved a chair over in front of the great armourial wardrobe, climbed up for a look on top of it, and there was the document.

It was the work of a moment to light the bedside candle, sit down in the chair, and find the passages which Mudge had said were marked.

"Why, the old something-or-other," I muttered almost admiringly. "Whatever made him think of that?"

At that moment I heard a sound that made my spectral heart skip a beat. Stealthy footsteps coming along the corridor.

Sliding the chair back to its place, pinching the candlewick hard with wet fingers to put it out and stop it from smoking, and slipping inside the wardrobe—all that took precious seconds, but I made it just before the door of the bedchamber opened. The wardrobe door had been slightly ajar, so I left it that way as I burrowed in behind the young duke's extensive wardrobe.

You may wonder why, upon hearing sounds outside, I did not simply vanish. You are forgetting I was still holding the document in my hand. I could hardly take it with me, nor could I very well leave it in the wardrobe. Only after I was inside did I start kicking myself—not quite literally, to be sure, for I was being very quiet in there. Why had I not thought to toss the document back up onto the top of the wardrobe?

But no, that wouldn't have done, anyway. It would have landed in complete disarray. Cecil would have known at once that someone had touched it, and I didn't want that.

But now what?

I could hear the swish of a heavy garment being taken off and thrown aside, and the scratch of a match as light flared in the room. It diminished, however, and died, and a young male voice muttered peevishly.

"This cursed dampness! Even the candle won't light!"

He tried again, and this time it caught feebly. Meanwhile I was suffering in the wardrobe. What if he decided to have another look at the document and make sure it was where he had hidden it? Wasn't that the first thing a normal young idiot would do in such circumstances?

The scrape of chair legs on the floor bore me out. Peeping through a space between a morning coat and a Prince Albert I could see enough through the slit in the door to know he was stepping up onto the chair. So it was now or never.

Just as he was saying "Good God! Where—?" I slipped the document through the crack in the door and let it fall to the floor.

My little ruse worked. Groping about the top in the dim light, he could see none too well what he was doing, and was completely taken in when he heard something hit the floor, besides which he was so relieved that nothing else mattered. He hopped down, picked up the document, and started breathing again.

"H'm. Must have brushed it off with my elbow," he muttered to himself. "Blast me if I'll put it up *there* again! Let me see . . . somewhere inside the wardrobe, perhaps . . ."

I did not wait for him to open the door. By the time he did so, I had vanished.

thirteen

WHEN I REENTERED the Tapestry Chamber, Lady Eleanore sat forward in her chair and eyed me eagerly.

"Success?"

"Of course."

"Good!"

"Cecil came back early and nearly surprised me, but not before I had gained the information we needed."

"He didn't see you?"

"Certainly not. It was a tight corner, but nothing I couldn't handle."

"Well, what did you find out?"

"You wouldn't believe it. The document was a copy of that mouldy old marriage contract form the dukes of Cheshire use, the one that's such a tradition with them. What ever made old Grubb think to get it out and read it through carefully is beyond me, but he did, and he found something in the fine print which will effectively prevent Cecil from proposing marriage again to our Virginia."

"Simon! You don't mean it!"

"I do. In fact, we should have thought of it ourselves, because the question came up at the time Piggy married Blister. It's the clause that stipulates that any bride of a duke of Cheshire must bring to her husband as part of her dowry a royal jewel, one that has once belonged to a king or queen of England."

Lady Eleanore stared at me, then laughed scornfully.

"Oh, that! But nobody's taken that seriously since—since before our time, even. Blister certainly didn't. He said, 'As long as Piggy brings me her three castles and four thousand gold sovereigns, the jewel can go hang!' "

"That's perfectly true. And every other duke of Cheshire within memory has waived the condition—but they were all of age and their own masters, or had guardians who didn't object. Cecil's guardians, however, are in a position to enforce the terms of the contract to the letter, and you may be sure they will."

Lady Eleanore heaved an exasperated sigh.

"What a shame! Well, this means the dear children will simply have to wait three years before they can become formally engaged—"

"A note was attached to the contract form which reminded Cecil that his guardians have control over his affairs until he reaches the age of thirty," I interrupted, dropping another bombshell.

"What?"

"The old duke, his father, was a very conservative man. He was seventy-one when Cecil was born, and had naturally come to the conclusion that no man has any sense before he has reached the age of thirty, if then. So . . . Do you expect Virginia to wait twelve years? No, it's a monstrous piece of bad luck. I still wonder what evil circumstance ever led old Grubb to recall that ridiculous clause and dig it out," I said, and then noticed Lady Eleanore was staring at me with the glittering eyes of one upon whom light has dawned.

"Well, I don't. I can guess exactly what it was," she declared, and from her bodice she drew forth a folded cutting from a newspaper.

"I've been meaning to show you this but hadn't got around to it because I thought other things were more important. Little did I know! Needless to say, it's caused a sensation everywhere, but nowhere more than here at Canterville Chase, I'll vow. It was the principal topic of conversation for most of the day."

She handed me the cutting. I unfolded it, and this is what I read:

ROYAL NECKLACE FOUND TO BE COUNTERFEIT
Famous "Henry VIII Rubies" Prove False

Mr Sherlock Holmes Has Been Called in on the Case

In the course of a routine examination of the Royal Collection in the Tower of London, the renowned gemologist Sir Lansing Carruthers has discovered that the famous "Henry VIII Rubies," a ruby necklace in an old Venetian setting, is a counterfeit.

"A masterpiece of forgery," Sir Lansing declared it to be.

Originally the property of Sir Alfred de Canterville, the first lord of that illustrious line, it might have remained so had he not worn it as a hatband at the coronation in 1509 of King Henry VIII, who happened to notice it and admire it.

Shortly thereafter word was conveyed to Sir Alfred at Canterville Chase that His Majesty was disposed to honour him by graciously accepting the ruby necklace as a token of Sir Alfred's loyalty and esteem.

After a delay of a month or so, Sir Alfred ran out of excuses, and turned over the necklace to the king's agents. After gracing the necks of several of Henry VIII's queens, including Anne Boleyn, the necklace eventually became a part of the royal collection of Crown Jewels in the Tower of London.

Now, however, it appears that the neckace is a counterfeit and the rubies are false. Authorities are at a loss to explain this sensational discrepancy, and Scotland Yard is being aided in its investigation by the celebrated detective, Mr Sherlock Holmes.

By the time I had concluded my perusal of this extraordinary report I was smiling grimly.

"The thick-witted fools! Inspector Lestrade must be handling the case for the Yard. You may be sure Mr. Holmes will quickly set them right. He will see the true answer to this 'sensational discrepancy,' just as I do. Wishing to make a show, Sir Alfred decorated his hat with false jewels, counting on the fact that no one was likely to observe them too closely on an occasion when everyone present would be ablaze with jewels. It was his bad luck that they happened to catch the king's eye.

"Then, when King Henry graciously offered to take them off his hands, he found himself in a tight corner. If they were discovered to be fake after he had given them to the king, that would be fatal. On the other hand, if he *said* they were fake when he handed them over, that would be worse than fatal. King Henry had a suspicious mind; he would never have believed such a story. He would have been sure Sir Alfred was trying to hold back the real rubies. Some unpleasant interrogation on the rack would have resulted. So Sir Alfred's only chance was to hand them over and hope for the best, and he took it. The old rascal! To think of it—Good Sir Alfred pawned off a fake on Bluff King Harry and got away with it! Now, that took some nerve!" I said proudly, finding in this deed of derring-do new cause for veneration of my noble great-grandfather and founder of the line.

"Indeed it did," agreed Lady Eleanore. "You're lucky your illustrious line wasn't cut off early, right at the neck. But there you are. I'm sure it was this newspaper story that made Lord Grubb remember there was something about royal jewels in the marriage contract form, and started him off to look for it."

"I'm sure you're right, my dear. Of all the bad timing! Why couldn't Sir Lansing Carruthers let well enough alone? Where do we go from here? Where can an American girl get hold of a royal jewel these days, no matter how rich her father may be? There simply aren't any available. . . . Wait a minute! How about Lady Poynton-Fentriss? She has an emerald ring that once belonged to George the Second!"

"She also has six marriageable daughters, and has her eye on Cecil for one of them—any one. I'll wager old Grubb has already made her privy to his discovery—they're related, you know—so you may be sure she's going to hang on to that emerald. She's not about to sell it to some upstart American Minister so that *his* daughter can cop the prize. Why, that ring is her ace in the hole now."

"A pox on her! Those daughters of hers are such frumps, too. . . . Could we steal it?"

"Oh, Simon, now you're just talking nonsense! You'd have Virginia winding up in gaol instead of church!"

"You're right, I'm maundering. But it does seem unfair. Hmm. So *that* is Cecil's sad secret! No wonder he's been acting so strangely toward Virginia. He feels he has to."

"Of course. I'm sure he'll end his visit here as soon as he decently can."

"No doubt. What rotten luck! That cursed newspaper story . . ."

For a while we brooded gloomily. But then, somewhat wryly, Lady Eleanore chuckled.

"Do you know who's the most excited of all the family about that story?"

"Who?"

"The twins. They've both read it about a dozen times, and Johnny has spent most of the day pawing through dime novels, because he's convinced it reminds him of something he read in one of them."

"Dime novels? What are those?"

"Penny dreadfuls—only the Americans call theirs dime novels. The twins have an enormous collection of them, all with the most lurid titles. Johnny's being very mysterious, and won't tell Ronny what he's looking for, so of course Ronny is reading them all again, too."

"Well, that's good. Keeps them quiet."

"Poor little tykes, they're having a bad time, though. They're worried about their sister. They can't understand why she's suddenly moping around. They came to me to ask a lot of questions, and I had to be very careful about what I said."

"Are you trying to tell me they have a good side to them?" I asked incredulously. She smiled.

"Nobody's all bad, Simon. They really do."

"Well, I suppose I'll have to believe it if you say so, but it's a strain. The twins. Hmm. Well, I don't think there's much *they* can do to help their sister at a time like this."

"I'm afraid not. But at least their hearts are in the right place."

After another period of silent meditation, Lady Eleanore

stirred in her chair and turned her eyes toward me with a sigh.

"Well, this hardly seems an appropriate time to talk about our selfish concerns, but I promised you I'd bring you news whenever it came, so I shall."

Needless to say, her words brought me bolt upright in my chair.

"News? What news?"

"There is a possibility of your leaving service here for a new position."

My heart bumped painfully in my chest.

"What—what kind of—"

"There is an opening just now for a ghost-at-large."

"Hurrah! Exactly what I wanted!"

"*But*—"

"I *knew* there would be a catch!"

"—before you will ever be permitted to leave Canterville Chase, you must first be officially declared dead and buried."

I was stunned.

"Dead? How can a ghost ever be dead?" I cried, stung by the patent impossibility of the conditions imposed. "Buried? How can I be buried when I don't even have a body in the usual sense? When I was struck by that bolt of lightning, the night I became a ghost, my body simply disappeared."

Lady Eleanore gave me the enigmatic look of a Delphic oracle.

"Those are a couple of wrinkles you'll have to iron out for yourself. You didn't suppose a cushy job like ghost-at-large would be laid in your lap without *some* effort on your part, did you?"

"*Some* effort? I might as well forget the whole idea," I retorted with a self-pitying groan.

"Well, that's up to you. Think it over. I just thought I'd tell you."

"Thanks for nothing!"

She gave me another enigmatic look, and rose from her chair.

"I must go back now and see what's up. There may be nothing we can do for those two poor young things, but we must try."

I gave her a melancholy look, and nodded. I might as well make the most of whatever activities came along at the Chase, because it was going to remain my home—and prison—forever and a day.

"Keep me posted," I muttered, and watched her go.

fourteen

GIVEN MY TEMPERAMENT, of course, I couldn't have stayed away from the action, no matter what my mood. Early next morning I was standing invisible watch on my favorite perch in the library under Good Sir Alfred's portrait. By now I was rather put out with the old fellow, having realized that if it were not for him, that story would never have appeared in the newspapers; and if the story had not appeared, Lord Grubb might never have remembered that infamous clause. I gave Sir Alfred a rather cold glance before settling myself atop the bookcase.

As usual, the first person to join me was Sheila, ready to continue her systematic polishing of the furniture; she seemed to be dedicated to doing every last stick in the room. And she had not been at work long before, as usual, her lovesick swain entered.

"Good morning, Sheila," he said in a low voice.

She glanced up, and the radiance of her smile made his face fire up like the stained-glass window. But then he quickly went pale again.

"Good morning, sir. . . . Why, what's the matter?"

He was looking so woebegone it alarmed her. She straightened up to face him as he crossed the room, stood before her, and burst out with a soft-spoken but heartfelt cry.

"I'm so miserable! I adore you!" he declared, and once again made a grab for her, almost as awkwardly as the first time. Still, there are grabs and there are grabs, and this one had a better air about it. At any rate, the smack he received this time was the kind he wanted. Sheila didn't *have* to turn up her face so obligingly, but she did. Her eyes widened, then closed, and she didn't draw away.

"Angel!" Wash murmured huskily against her cheek, and then kissed her again. And this time her arms slowly went round his neck, and a trim ankle came into view as one leg bent back from the knee.

"You've got a live one there, my boy," I murmured approvingly to myself.

At last, however, Sheila recovered her wits and pushed him away.

"Oh, sir, you mustn't do that!" she said breathlessly. "Taking advantage of a poor servant girl—it's shameful!"

"I don't want to take advantage of you, I just want to kiss you!" said Wash, and he did it again. But then a familiar sound in the hall made them spring apart. Young people never learn; they *knew* a creature of habit such as the Minister would be turning up at any moment with his morning newspaper, and yet they took chances. Her pretty face flaming, Sheila snatched up her cloths and polish and whisked out of the room in one direction as the Minister entered in the other, whilst poor addled Wash dropped to his knees and stared wildly at the floor. His father stopped in the doorway, his eyes busy and his lips pursed severely, then bore down on the lad.

"May I ask what you are doing, Washington?"

"Er—just checking up on the bloodstain, Pa."

"Indeed? Well, you are looking in the wrong place. It happens to be over there by the fireplace."

"Oh—er—does it? Oh, yes, so it is! I—uh—"

"Washington."

"Sir?"

"Have you been molesting that young parlourmaid?"

"*Molesting* her?" Wash sprang indignantly to his feet. "I wouldn't *think* of molesting her!"

"Umm. Good," said the Minister, a bit startled by the heat of his son's response. "I won't have you getting a servant in trouble. It's not the American way. If you're going to pick up any English customs, pick up some good ones. Mind, I don't altogether blame you. You're only human, and the girl's as tasty a little piece of goods as I've seen in—"

"Pa! I won't have her spoken of in those terms!" cried Wash in a choking voice, and he rushed out of the room.

His father stared after him, then plumped down in an armchair with his newspaper forgotten on his knees.

"Good God!" said Minister Otis, and for once I was almost sorry for him.

In fact, it never ceases to amaze me when I see how magnanimous a person such as myself can be. Here was one of my former tormentors, young Wash, in a mess up to his ears; I should have been gloating over his misfortunes; but instead, while watching his bumbling operations with Sheila, I found myself a prey to sneaking affection for the pup, found myself rooting for him! And not only that, here I was putting myself in the Minister's shoes and watching *him* sympathetically instead of maliciously when, moments later, he rose and slowly trudged out of the room.

I was about to leave it myself when Johnny came pacing

in, hands behind his back in a posture quite unnatural for one of his years, and with Ronny right behind him squawking indignantly.

"Aw, come on, that's not fair! Tell me!"

Johnny stopped, swung around, and gave his brother a glance of knowing superiority.

"I shall reveal all when the time comes. Until then, my lips are sealed," he said, employing words that must have come straight out of one of those dime novels of theirs. He eyed his brother arrogantly. "You read them, same as I did. Surely you must have noticed something."

"But which book was it in?" shrilled poor Ronny.

Johnny's eyes darted about, narrowed to slits.

"It is best not to mention that just yet. There are spies everywhere," he muttered, speaking more truth than he knew; and out he went by another door, pursued by his suffering sibling.

I watched them go with a sardonic eye, then slid down from my perch and drifted away back to the Tapestry Chamber, reviewing the state of affairs as I went. First it was Virginia, and now Wash, both of them bogged down on the road to romance, and who was to help them? Not the twins, certainly; as potential Cupids they had the right build but not the know-how. No, what the situation needed was a take-charge type, a dynamic mover and shaker; and in looking around for candidates at Canterville Chase, I could see only one possibility: myself. The mastermind of Cousin Henry's Night would have to do it again. Lacking the presence of the world's greatest problem-solver, the person best qualified to straighten out a muddle of these proportions was I. I must bear the burden. As I returned to the Tapestry Chamber, the question uppermost in my mind was "What would Sherlock Holmes do?"

The best way to find out was by emulating his methods. Selecting a battered old briar from my pipe rack, and filling a pouch with an ounce of strong shag tobacco, I hunted up a box of matches and was ready.

"The game's afoot," I muttered to myself. "I shall spend whatever time is necessary in the deepest concentration, and I shall not desist until I have a plan of action."

And with that, once again it was down, down, down. Soon I was seated on the well-worn headsman's block, staring with vacant eyes at Robin Clump while thick wreaths of rank tobacco smoke swirled round my head.

For a while I accomplished nothing other than a coughing spell brought on by the pungent weed. That jewel business, now, and Good Sir Alfred's daring deception. A feeling was growing in the back of my mind that something was wrong with my analysis there, but nothing seemed to come of it. My eyes went to the tracery of bones that had been Robin Clump, and I was moved to address them.

"Ah, Robin, if only you could speak! You lived in Good Sir Alfred's time. It might be that you could unravel mysteries which are a closed book to me."

Perhaps you are expecting to hear that a spirit voice answered me from the gaping jaw of Robin's skull. Well, don't be silly. A skeleton like Robin's is a pile of bones and nothing more. And yet, I will admit, as I did when describing an earlier visit to his digs, I always found his silent companionship a source of inspiration.

Somehow my thoughts stopped milling about aimlessly and began to fall into line. I found myself trying to recall likely sources of information about Good Sir Alfred, and as I did so I felt a severe twinge of filial guilt.

My father's memoirs!

He had entrusted them to me with the solemn injunction that they were to be passed along in manuscript for a few generations and not be published until a good safe hundred years or so had passed. After his death, when I had a thousand things on my mind, I had given them a hurried reading and had swiftly concluded that a hundred years thence would be quite soon enough to risk publication. I had visited a little-used lumber room—what Americans would call an attic—high in the old wing of the Chase, and had hidden the manuscript under floorboards there, with the intention of passing along its whereabouts to my eldest son when he came of age. But then when I suddenly disappeared and went through such dramatic changes in my existence, I never gave the matter another thought until now.

Some of my father's best stuff, I recalled, had been anecdotes about his famous grandfather. For instance, wasn't there something about Sir Alfred luring a visiting Venetian goldsmith from London to Canterville Chase with promises of short hours and high pay? Yes, by George—Luca da Ponterialto had been the fellow's name. Sir Alfred had made much of him for a while. But then, legend would have it, Luca was suddenly seen no more and was gone as if vanished from the face of the earth. No one ever seemed to have known exactly what did happen to him.

Of course, knowing my revered ancestor's business methods, I had a suspicion that his Venetian goldsmith was somewhere not far from where I was sitting at that very moment, in the same sort of place I wished I had put my Venetian. But why would Sir Alfred set Luca to work on some project or other and then end their association with such extreme measures?

To keep him from talking, of course! Sir Alfred had

prevailed upon the fellow to create a magnificent counterfeit to be worn at the Coronation, and then made sure he
would keep quiet about it.

Yes, that must be it. Or . . . or was it? Again, some
sort of conflicting opinion was stirring in the back of my
mind. Something was not quite right, and I could not rest
until I had made certain it was not something important.

So it was up, up, up this time, up to the lumber room.
When finally I returned to the Tapestry Chamber, I was
covered with the cobwebs and dust of centuries, but I
had what I wanted.

Skimming through the yellowed pages, I soon found the
passage I was looking for, and in reading it discovered that
my memory had been accurate except for one small detail.
That detail, however, was enough to make my brain whirl
in its socket and start reversing directions.

My father made it quite clear that Good Sir Alfred had
engaged the services of Luca da Ponterialto immediately
after the Coronation, not before!

From that moment on, my father had the sort of reader
every author dreams of—a reader hanging on his every
word.

The next significant anecdote I came upon was one I
must have missed in that first hasty skim-through three
centuries earlier, because I did not remember it at all. My
father told it at great length, with many details of purely
local interest, and rather than try to recall his somewhat
archaic prose, I shall paraphrase it:

Good Sir Alfred had his eccentricities, of course, like
anyone else, and was not the only noble lord who had ever

arranged for his own coffin to be constructed while he was still alive; but one thing, in his case, had always seemed slightly bizarre.

It seems that one day when the coffin was nearly completed, Sir Alfred declared his intention of lining it personally with black velvet. Ordering the workmen out of their shop, he worked like a demon for the better part of a day, cutting cloth, sewing seams, and hammering tacks. The workmen later declared they could not have done a neater job themselves. Of course, they would have said that anyway, but one had a feeling they meant it.

Once I had read this passage, I did not have to look further. Almost instantly I was recalling my great-grandfather's famous last words, that cryptic utterance which had puzzled generations of historians. Just as he was breathing his last, surrounded by his grieving family and faithful retainers, he opened one eye, gave vent to a mischievous chuckle, and rumbled, "Who sayest thou canst not take it with thee?"

Plodding, step-by-step deduction is all very well for journeyman work, but your true genius goes far beyond that. His great secret is that sudden flash of intuition in which everything becomes blindingly clear.

A plan had unfolded in my mind with the brilliancy of a peacock's tail—and it was a plan that went much farther than one might think.

fifteen

THE REST OF THE DAY was a trial to me, for although there was so much to be done it made my head swim, none of it could be done before nightfall; so there was nothing for it but to wait.

Never had I looked forward with such eagerness to Lady Eleanore's nightly visit. When she finally appeared I was so exhilarated I seized her in my arms and gave her a hearty buss.

"Simon!" She pushed me away with a breathless little laugh. "Whatever is the matter with you?"

"Elly, I've got it! I've got the whole lot wrapped up in one big bundle! Sit down. No, here take the *best* chair, dear. I'm too excited to sit, anyway. Now, to begin with . . ."

I showed her my father's memoirs, and read her the pertinent passages, as Mudge would have called them. By the time I finished, her eyes were shining as hopefully as mine.

"Those last words of his, now," I said when I had concluded my readings. "Which of his many precious possessions might he have been referring to when he said those words? Which would he treasure above all others? I say, the one he risked his life for!"

"Of course!"

"Very well, then. So I hardly need tell you what our first step must be," I said, and proceeded nonetheless to explain it. Lady Eleanore was quick to agree.

"Then we'll meet at midnight to test my theory," I said. "Be sure to bring the necessary equipment I mentioned. As for the rest of my plan, there's much to be done. For one thing, I must have a diamond ring."

"A diamond ring? Why?"

I explained the rest of my plan. She stared at me, and sat back shaking her head in amazement.

"Mad, mad, mad," she breathed. "Still, it just might work."

"It's got to! Now, how about Mrs. Otis? Surely she must have some diamonds among her jewellery."

Lady Eleanore shook her head.

"So far as I know—and I've had a look, just out of feminine curiosity—the only diamonds she has are in the rings she wears. You can't very well creep into the master bedroom and strip one off her finger, now can you?"

"But I *must* have—"

"Wait a minute! The young duke has one."

"What? Cecil?"

"Yes. That's another thing I learned from his valet. Cecil brought along a diamond solitaire, hoping to put it to good use. I believe it's in the waistcoat pocket of his grey suit."

"The one with the pinstripes and the narrow lapels?"

"Yes."

"I'll get it!"

"But what if he misses it in the morning?"

"I'll return it before then."

"Well, all right. But are you sure you can find that passage—"

138

"Yes! It will mean an hour or two in the library after we've finished with our errand, but I'm sure I can remember which book it's in once I have a chance to search the shelves."

"All right, then. I can tell you one thing, we had *better* move fast. You haven't heard the latest development."

"What's that?"

"Mr. Holmes and Dr. Watson are coming tomorrow."

"No!"

"Yes. They will arrive at the Ascot railway station on the 10:40 morning train from London."

I can assure you this message seemed to transmit itself into dots and dashes straight up my spine. Yet side by side with consternation went a strangely stimulating thrill of satisfaction.

"I knew it!" I said. "Trust him not to go baying off after a false scent. He won't be far behind us. Let us not forget that he has been very successful with jewels."

"Yes, indeed. What's more, I have learned that Lord Canterville is coming, too—in fact, it was he who asked Mr. Holmes to take a hand in the case."

It was with a mystic sense of exaltation that I turned and looked down at Lady Eleanore.

"So!" I murmured. "The time has come at last, as I always knew it would someday—the time when I shall have to pit my wits against the greatest detective of them all, Mr. Sherlock Holmes!"

"It looks that way."

"Well, I can't begin operations until everyone in the house has retired. That will give us twelve hours before he arrives on the scene. Everything must be accomplished before that time."

Lady Eleanore stood up.

"Do you think we can do it, Simon?"

"We can only try!" I told her, and took her again into my arms. Her lips were soft, and her body melted against mine—till suddenly she sprang back with a cry.

"Simon!" she gasped. "I can't believe it!"

"Elly!" I cried. "It's a special dispensation!"

For an instant she stood transfixed. Then, seductively, Lady Eleanore returned to my arms.

"Let's make sure," said she.

It was a new ghost who walked the corridors of Canterville Chase that night, a ghost who, in perhaps an unprecedented way, had reestablished contact with an important condition of humanity, and my whole viewpoint was changed. Gone were old grudges; I simply longed now to see everyone in the world happily paired off. I not only wished connubial bliss for Virginia and her young duke, I hoped that Wash would gather his rosebud while he might. I was everybody's friend.

When I reached the main corridor that led to the family bedrooms and the principal guest rooms, a welcome silence greeted me. Everyone had retired to rest.

Despite my euphoria, I was careful to keep a sharp eye out for any strings stretched across the passage or nutshells strewn on the floor (another of the twins' tricks), since I still could not bring myself quite to trust them. But nothing of that sort impeded my progress. It was without incident that I gained the door of the Royal Bedchamber.

Though I entered with the greatest caution, I was not afraid of rousing the young duke. Lads of his age sleep like logs, I reminded myself. When I was able to observe him as he lay dreaming away under the great feathered canopy of the stately bed, I felt certain I could proceed with safety. Furthermore, the way I came and went, the place was beginning to be familiar territory.

One would think the appurtenances of a Royal Bed-chamber would be kept in proper repair, but standards, now that beheading by royal decree had gone out of fashion, were no longer what they once were. During my previous visit I had come to understand that the door of the great armourial wardrobe was ajar simply because the catch no longer worked properly. And this time, when I eased it open, it creaked alarmingly. With my heart in my throat I froze, and waited. Apart from stirring restlessly and flopping over onto his stomach, however, Cecil continued to slumber.

Now it was a question of pawing through his clothing, looking for the grey suit with the pinstripes and the narrow lapels. At last I found it. My trembling fingers sought the waistcoat pockets, and in the second one pinched together on the hard, cold facets of a large gem. I drew it forth, and saw I was holding a diamond solitaire ring of truly ducal proportions, especially for so young a duke. It occurred to me to wonder how the scalawag had managed to provide himself with so expensive a persuader, but any such speculation was a side issue just then. Besides, at that very instant something happened that scattered my thoughts like chaff before the wind.

Cecil whirled in his bed like a top and sat straight up crying, "No, no, Lord Grubb, I will *not* return to Eton!"

Of all times to have a nightmare, he had picked the worst! With a reaction more human than ghostly, I dropped to the floor and slid under the bed.

Well, it seemed as if every last person at Canterville Chase, including Miss Virginia, came running down the corridor and into the young duke's room within the next thirty seconds. Fuming amid the dust and cobwebs under the bed—those maids would *have* to be given a good dressing-down!—I listened helplessly while everyone tried to console the young duke and assure him he had merely had a nightmare, and while Cecil (blushing, no doubt) responded with vague and misleading answers as to the contents of his dream. At any instant, watching the twin's feet scamper about, I expected to find myself in an eyeball-to-eyeball confrontation with them when for some reason they decided to look under the bed.

After a moment Mrs. Otis left the room and returned shortly with an announcement which did not surprise me in the least.

"Sir," she said, "here is an efficacious remedy I hope you will try. It is called Dr. Dobell's tincture. It is remarkably successful in combatting a variety of malaises, insomnia being among them. One spoonful of this, and you will sleep like a babe."

Docilely the young duke allowed himself to be dosed. I squeezed my eyes shut at the sheer horror of it, but what could I do?

After what seemed an interminable time, Cecil was finally tucked into bed, and everybody left. Somewhere a mellow-throated clock tolled the third quarter of the hour. I longed to groan a churchyard groan, though of course that would have been inadvisable. Much more of this and I would be late for my midnight tryst with Lady Eleanore!

It may be you are beginning to consider me an easily panicked ghost. Why, you may be wondering, did I not pull myself together and vanish through the wainscotting the instant Cecil stirred?

The answer is that I had a special problem on my hands which precluded any such vanishing. Oh, I could have vanished, all right—but what about the ring I was clutching? A diamond is the hardest substance known to man. It was one thing to thin oneself out to the vanishing point, but just you try to thin out a diamond and see how far you get. No, I had to escape from the room by conventional means, and soon.

Above me Cecil seemed to be settling down, and I was about to wriggle out from under the bed when the door opened again and someone tiptoed in, causing me to withdraw like a startled snail into its shell.

"Cecil?"

The bedsprings bounced violently, menacing my head, as Cecil sat up again.

"Ginny! What are you doing here?" he asked, rather hopefully, I thought. All this in whispers, of course.

"Oh, Cecil!" She sounded close to tears. "I *have* to know what is troubling you and—and why you have been so distant! Is it something I have done?"

Well, as you might imagine, that was all it took to break down the reserve of anyone as susceptible as the young duke. In no time at all it was "Oh, no, my angel, how could you do *anything* that would— I mean to say— Well, dash it all, you know I love you, and there is nothing I want to do more than ask you to be mine, only . . ."

Then the whole story about the fatal clause in the marriage contract was poured out, and after asking each other what they could do about it, and agreeing that they had to do something but didn't know what, the young lovers fell silent and sat side by side and doubtless hand in hand on the edge of the bed. I began to hope fervently that Miss Virginia had really received as proper an upbringing as Lady Eleanore felt she had. If those two became any more impulsive, I might *never* get away. I longed to cry out "I'm all for love, children, but *not now!*" Upbringing told, however, and after a few ecstatic kisses, Virginia rose to go.

"Now, you stay in bed in the morning, poor boy, and don't even *think* of getting up for our ride in the park," she ordered happily. "I'll go for a trot by myself. I know now that it isn't because you don't care for my company."

"Care? You know nothing is more precious to me! I long to propose to you again, and if you don't believe it, I can even show you something that will prove it! Wait, I'll get it, it's in my waistcoat pocket . . ."

Beneath the bed, one who was already pale as a ghost turned even paler. Now there would be another outcry, and—

"No, don't you dare!" Virginia's voice was low but intense. "I don't want to see—whatever it is—until I can—I mean—"

Despite her growing incoherence, Cecil caught enough of the drift of the objections to bow to them.

"Oh, very well. Perhaps you're right. Well . . . Goodnight, my beloved!"

"Good-night, my prince!"

"Duke."

"Duke, prince—I love you both!"

The door closed, but still I held my breath. Would Cecil be moved to take a sentimental look at the ring anyway, now that the subject had come up? For a moment there was no sound except for his heavy breathing. Then, after an eternity, he turned and came back to bed. But it was some time before his respiration became regular enough to allow me to escape.

sixteen

OU'RE LATE!"

"I know—but wait till you hear what I've learned!" Like any husband late for an appointment with his wife, I was glad of a chance to offer a distraction. "It's just what we needed. Virginia has ordered Cecil to stay in bed tomorrow morning and catch up on his sleep. She will be riding alone."

"But—but—do you mean to say they've gotten everything straightened out between them?"

"Yes, indeed. They made up, and I thought I'd never get away."

"Simon! You don't mean—"

"No, no, Virginia was a good girl, but they had a nice little talk on the bed—"

"What?"

"On the *edge* of the bed, that is to say. Listen, we haven't time for this now, I'll tell you all about it later."

"Simon, you are maddening! However . . . well, if that's the way things stand now, I'm sure Cecil will show up for their ride anyway."

"Not a chance. Mrs. Otis called Dr. Dobell in on the case. Cecil will be lucky if he can totter out of the house before noon."

"What on earth happened?"

I gave her a quick résumé.

"So Virginia will be alone, Elly, and the only problem now will be to steer her in the right direction."

"Leave that to me."

Our meeting place was the Canterville family burial ground. From the center of the large plot rose the massive, shadowy outlines of the ancient crypt which held the remains of the immediate family, whilst round it were scattered the mounds and gravestones of poor relations. A new moon had long ago sunk from view in the west; overhead a few stars twinkled feebly through scudding clouds. A chill wind tossed the foliage of two large weeping willows, which drooped with appropriate melancholy over the dismal scene.

"Let us make up for lost time," urged Lady Eleanore, and together we hurried to the door of the crypt. When we tugged it open, the sable blackness of the tomb seemed to rush out at us like a puff of air from some nameless creature suffering from bad breath.

"Did you bring the crowbar, Elly?"

"Yes. Did you bring a dark lantern?"

"A dark lantern? I thought you were going to bring one."

"I thought *you* were. You never said anything about my bringing one."

"I thought I did."

"Well, you didn't. Drat! What will we do now? I can't see a hand before my face."

"Never mind, I'll provide the light. Feel your way inside and I'll follow."

Once inside with the door shut, I began to emit a greenish phosphorescent glow of the sort I had used with considerable effect on numerous haunting occasions.

"Well, you're no lantern, but you're better than nothing," said Lady Eleanore crossly. She stooped to peer at the nameplate on the nearest coffin. "Can you turn up your glow a bit? I can scarcely read a word of any of these names."

"Don't bother. The first earl isn't up here in the Johnny-come-lately section," I reminded her. "He's well toward the back."

We crept through the crypt with cautious steps, and Lady Eleanore nodded.

"I'm sure you're right. These coffins are becoming mouldier and mouldier."

"Look." I pointed to a large coffin that stood against the center of the rear wall. "There it is."

At first the nameplate on the venerable sarcophagus was completely illegible, but once we had scraped a crusted layer of dried green slime from its surface, we were able to make it out:

ALFRED
Le sieur de Canterville
1513

"Now then, the crowbar!"

I expected the better part of four centuries to have taken their toll, but I had not reckoned with the wood of Old England. The coffin was made of stout English oak, and was still full of heart, still ready to fight off invasion. Try as I might, I could not jimmy open the lid. Lady Eleanore strove to help, but to no avail. Panting from the exertion, I finally stopped and faced our problem squarely.

"What we need is two crowbars."

"I wish you'd thought of that in the first place."

"How was I to know the thing would be so hard to open? Dearest, nip back to the toolshed and fetch another one, will you?"

"I suppose I'll have to," she grumbled.

"And hurry!"

Lady Eleanore picked her way to the door, pushed it open enough to slip outside, and sped away on her errand. I fidgeted for a moment or two and then, as one always does in such situations, decided to have one more go at that lid while I was waiting. And as you might know, suddenly it uttered a long ratchety creak of defeat and came open. With a happy cry I pushed up the lid until it lay back against the wall.

Normally I might have considered this business of prising open the final resting place of my own great-grandfather to be in bad taste; but in the circumstances, I had scarcely an instant's revulsion. There lay the sacred bones of the first earl, the ponderous skull grinning up at me with the same benevolent expression he must have worn in life, but there was no time for bowing of head or other customary hypocrisies. I was too busy stripping away the worm-riddled shreds of black velvet that still covered the inner surfaces of the coffin.

After a mercifully brief interval of groping about, I had the exquisite thrill of feeling my fingers close round a flat rectangular object.

I drew out a small box whose velvet cover was as stiff and cracked as the velvet that had concealed it. Carefully I opened the crumbly case, and there in the greenish glow of my phosphorescence, a circle of gems responded dully to the light.

Of course the combination of green on red made them

look rather grey, but there was no doubt about it: they were rubies.

The only thing that marred my triumph was not having Lady Eleanore there to share it. I could hardly wait for her return. Noticing that she had left the door ajar, I decided it might be prudent to turn off the juice for the moment and wait in darkness till I heard her coming. I doubted that any of the greenish glow would reach the crack in the doorway, but there was no sense in taking chances.

After a few endless moments, I heard cautious footsteps approaching outside, and was about to call out a jaunty greeting when some sixth sense advised caution. In the next instant I heard voices.

"Coo! Look—the door's open!"

"Golly! Shall we go in?"

"Of course! We have to—just like in the book, where they went into the . . ."

"The what?"

"Come in and I'll tell you!"

The door creaked open wider. Footsteps scuffed inside.

"Coo! It's dark! Smells bad, too!"

"Light the lantern!"

I don't mind admitting it now, those twins had a way of rattling me. I felt I couldn't vanish and leave the rubies where they might find them, but I couldn't just stand there, either. The only way I could think of to get out of sight quickly was to leap up and stretch out in the coffin on top of Sir Alfred.

As usual, of course, I forgot my current condition. In this case I forgot I was pretty well firmed up. As a result there was a slight click or two as I displaced a couple of bones.

"Hey! What was that?"

"I didn't hear anything."

"Well, I did!"

"Aw, you're a sissy!"

"I am not! But light the lantern!"

"I'm going to!"

Considerable scratching of matches followed, and finally a dim and fitful light threw into relief the rough surfaces of the crypt above my head.

"All right! Now we're here! Now tell me!"

"All right, I will."

"Which book was it?"

"*The Secret of Pirates' Cave!*"

"*The Secret of . . . Pirates' Cave?*"

"Sure! Remember how the pirates were always buried in their special secret cave on Crossbones Island?"

"Sure I do! But—"

"And remember how Jasper Dane, the pirate captain, was buried there, too?"

"Sure! But—"

"And remember how the Spanish governor tried to get the Golden Crown of the Incas away from Jasper Dane but Jasper Dane fooled him by giving him a false crown and had the real crown buried with him in the cave?"

"Say!"

"Get it?"

"Sure I do!"

"Isn't this place like a cave?"

"Sure!"

"And wasn't ol' Al the head of the Cantervilles?"

"Sure!"

"Well, all right then! I'll bet that's what he did with that necklace! So all we've got to do is find out where he's buried in here and I'll bet we'll find the real necklace!"

By this time, of course, my forehead was bathed in cold perspiration and I was cursing every hack who ever wrote a dime novel. Once again the twins were proving too much for me, and this time they truly had me cornered.

"Johnny, you're right! C'mon, let's look for ol' Al! I wonder which one he's in?"

"Well, he was the big cheese of this whole outfit, so he must have the biggest coffin. . . . Lookee! There's a great big one back there!"

"Golly, yes—and it's already open!"

In another moment the twins would climb up and stare inside and find me there—and that, I was sure, would be too much for them despite all their solemn promises of good behaviour. But before I had to face that embarrassment, the light flickered on the ceiling above me, and suddenly the crypt was pitch black again.

"Darn this lantern, it's gone out!"

"Well, light it again!"

During that brief interval I had gotten hold of myself and begun to think. According to Lady Eleanore, the little monsters did have a better side to their natures, at least where their sister was concerned. Could I possibly appeal to it? Supposedly they were fond of Virginia, and worried about her. Might I not do better simply to let them in on the secret and explain how important the rubies might be to their sister?

On the other hand, Johnny was getting nowhere with the lantern. What if he used up all his matches? Then surely they would have to give up and leave, at least long enough to fetch more matches, and I would be safe. I held my breath and hoped for the best. My position, I might add, was extremely uncomfortable. Sir Alfred's skeleton was the nearest thing to a bed of nails I should ever care to lie on. His bones prodded me viciously as though he actively resented supporting a great-grandson. And then all at once, just when I thought I might yet rid myself of the twins, one of my progenitor's rib bones cracked under me with a sound like a pistol shot.

Twin gasps acknowledged the sound.

"What was that?"

Now there was nothing to do but reveal myself. And since it was obvious that if I were going to do so, I would have to provide the illumination for our interview personally, I switched on my greenish glow and slowly sat up in the coffin.

"Good evening, boys."

I spoke in a tone of voice that was positively avuncular —and got the surprise of my entire existence. The house, it seemed, was one thing—the crypt, another. Two small faces, so pale that they reflected only the faintest tinge of green, turned up to me, and two pairs of eyes bulged alarmingly.

"Ai! It's Im!" they cried with one voice, and stampeded to the door and outside in a blur of tingling flesh.

At first I sat there, too astonished to move, and watched them go. Then, as the truth dawned on me, I vaulted out of the coffin and began an uproarious jig of triumph.

"Simon, what are you *doing*?"

I had not even heard her enter. I stopped and flung my arms wide.

"Elly! I did it! I finally did it! I scared the *whey* out of the twins!"

"Is *that* what happened? I thought I saw those two imps running toward the house, and wondered what they were up to. Oh, good grief, now they'll probably rouse the whole household! Simon, we've got to hurry!"

"Never mind, I've already found the rubies."

"*What?*"

"I'll explain later. Help me with this lid." I turned back to the coffin and peered inside at its occupant. "Well, sir, you certainly did take it with you for quite a while, but all good things must come to an end."

"It's all his fault, anyway."

"You're quite right, my dear."

With somewhat indecent haste we slammed down the lid of the coffin in his face and left Good Sir Alfred to mourn his losses.

"Bring that lantern the twins dropped."

"I've got it."

"Good. Now let's get out of here, because I still have a long night ahead of me. You that way, I this!" I said, and with a hasty kiss we parted.

Moments later I was in the library, ready to begin Phase Three.

This part of the operation proved to be still more time-consuming.

I don't know whether you are a compulsive and omnivorous reader, as I am, but if you are you will understand my plight. Whenever the family was away, most of my waking hours had been spent in the library. In the course of three hundred years, I must have read every book in the huge collection; but like so many avid readers, a day or two after I have finished the average book, I could not tell you the name of the author or the title if my continuing existence depended on it.

I knew the book I wanted was there somewhere, but I could not recall a thing about it except that it contained the passage I wanted to put my hands on. I had the feeling it was the sort of book that found its way to the topmost, least accessible shelves of a large private library: one of those books any sensible household would have given to a charity bazaar long ago. Apart from that I could recall nothing about it.

Closing all the doors, I lit two lamps and went to work. For a while I poked about the shelves in an unsystematic fashion, hoping something would ring a bell. I must have run up and down the twelve-foot library ladder fifty times, and finally unfirmed myself a good bit in order to make the effort less wearing. From below the stained-glass window, the portrait of Good Sir Alfred seemed to glare at me with unusual ferocity, and I confess I found myself unable to meet his eyes.

Then after a while I bethought me of my great adversary, Sherlock Holmes, and said to myself, "All right, now, stop all this scatterbrained activity, sit down and *think!*"

It was the thing to do, of course. A quarter hour of intense concentration brought a breakthrough that narrowed the field drastically, and also left me feeling especially foolish.

"Of course!" I told myself, "I remember now! Of all things, it was some sort of—of ghost story!"

The recovery of this helpful clue gave me renewed energy. But where would that particular ghost story be? Despite the well-deserved popularity of this genre, my memory still insisted that the book was to be found in the upper boondocks, so it was back up the ladder and the whole thing to do over again.

As I searched, another clue fought through to consciousness. It had been written by the vicar of some obscure country parish. Running my finger past Doddridge's *Ser-*

mons; My Thirty Years Among the Swahilis by Reverend
C. Adolphus Stoop; and *Christian Thoughts for Today* by
Reverend Timothy Blenkinsop, I suddenly came to a small,
dusty, badly bound volume authored by the Reverend
Judson Hodgins and entitled *The Wraith of Wrackley
Mill*.

"That's it! No, it can't be! Still, it might!" I said to myself, and pulled the book out of its place with such reckless
zeal that I went over backwards and tumbled off the ladder
to the floor.

In my moderately unfirm condition, I did not fall with
much force or make much noise. The book was less fortunate. It landed with a smash and lay open beside me with
a broken back. I reached for it—and there, gleaming up at
me—a lucky omen, surely!—was the very passage I had been
searching for.

Taking it up tenderly, and extinguishing the lamps, I
sped back to the Tapestry Chamber, where I was again
hard at work for the better part of two hours. It was day-
break before I finally tumbled into bed. Somewhere in the
distance a cock crew.

"Go to, thou naughty fowl," I murmured with a smile,
and fell into an exhausted sleep.

seventeen

THE NEXT SOUND I heard was a rap on the door.

"Yes?"

"Get ready, Simon."

"Right away!"

Lady Eleanore's steps receded. Shaking myself awake, I rose and dressed with care. Whilst putting the finishing touches to my attire, I looked out my window and there across the park came Miss Virginia, her little pony moving at a sedate trot through the brilliant sunshine of a splendid morning. Closer and closer to the house she came, until I began to grow concerned.

"Don't fail me now, Elly!" I muttered anxiously.

I should have known better. All at once the most extraordinary assemblage of large black clouds came rushing together from all directions, out of nowhere, and began elbowing each other like toughs in a barroom, directly over Virginia's head.

The result was the fiercest one-minute cloudburst it has been my privilege to witness. For sixty seconds it raged, after which the skies became as cloudless and peaceful as ever, leaving Virginia in much the same condition Reckless

Rupert and I had been in after our visit to the Blue Bed-chamber.

From the house came hurrying the angular figure of Mrs. Umney.

"Mercy me, just see what's happened to our poor girl! Why, she's drenched to the skin!"

"Yes, and look at my hair!" wailed Virginia, brushing sodden tresses out of her eyes. "It's horrid!"

"Well, now, we wouldn't want a certain young man to see us looking like this, would we?" said Mrs. Umney. "Just you go round the old east wing there and take the back stairs, dearie, and that way you can return to your room through the back passage without being seen."

Thus it was that Virginia rode her pony round to the rear of the old east wing, turned it loose there to find its way to the stables, and came up the back staircase. And thus it was she passed a secret door that had been left ajar, and peeping inside saw a melancholy figure seated in a despairing attitude in an old armchair.

I hope you will read Oscar Wilde's account of Virginia's visit to the Tapestry Chamber. By this point in his narrative the information had become extremely sketchy; either that or he simply decided to tailor events to suit his own tastes as an author. Oscar always was headstrong. At any rate, what actually happened was quite different from his version.

"Oh, it's you!" said Virginia, after staring at me briefly and without the slightest fear—she was a natural-born ghost-accepter. Then she noticed the blazing fire I had thoughtfully provided in the grate of my fireplace, and added, "May I come in? I'm absolutely drenched!"

"By all means, please do!" I sprang up to escort her to a spot in front of the fireplace, where I had her stand with her back close to it, in order to dry out her riding habit. As a result she was enveloped in a veritable cloud of steam during the whole of our conversation, giving the Tapestry Chamber the atmosphere of a Chinese hand laundry. But then I could hardly have taken her where we were going in such a damp condition; she would have caught her death of a cold.

"Well! So this is where you live, is it?" she said, glancing round with that fine freedom in her large blue eyes.

"If you can call it living," I replied, remembering to resume my melancholy air.

"Poor thing, you do look wretched. I should have expected to find you more cheerful, after the great success you had with Cousin Henry. We're ever so grateful."

"It did go off well, didn't it?" Resisting an impulse to gossip about Cousin Henry for a moment and have a few laughs, I forced myself back into the melancholy mould. "And yet, I am not happy."

"Is it your conscience that is bothering you? I know, of course, that you have been very wicked."

"What do you mean, wicked? If anyone has been wicked, it's those little brothers of yours!"

"The twins? Why, you almost scared them to death last night!"

I chuckled vainly.

"I suppose they woke up the entire household—"

"No, only me."

"Only you?"

"They didn't dare tell Mama and Papa they'd been running around outside after midnight, but they had to tell someone, so they came in and shook me awake. What were you doing down there in that awful place, anyway?"

"Never mind, nothing wicked—I was merely getting a little of my own back."

"Now, don't pretend you're not wicked, because Mrs. Umney told us, the first day we arrived here, that you had killed your wife."

"*That* old chatterbox!"

"Your wife?"

"Mrs. Umney."

"Well, *did* you kill your wife?"

"Well, yes, but it was a purely family matter, and concerned no one else."

"What a terrible thing to say! It is *wrong* to kill anyone."

"You didn't know *her*. My wife was very plain, never had my ruffs properly starched, and knew nothing about cookery. Why, there was a buck I had shot in Hogley Woods, a magnificent pricket, and do you know how she had it sent up to table? I shall spare you the details. Wrong, indeed! And when it comes to that," I went on, seeing the opening I had been waiting for, "if we're going to be nicey-nicey about things, I don't think it was very nice of her brothers to starve me to death, even though I did kill her."

"Starve you to death? Oh, that's dreadful! Is *that* your trouble? Are you hungry? If you are, I can bring you some delicious chicken soup. Mrs. Umney sees to it that cook always has some ready for anyone who—"

"Cook? Mrs. Umney makes the chicken soup herself!"

"Does she really? Well, it's awfully good."

I smiled at the dear girl.

"Virginia, I must say you're quite nice. Altogether different from the rest of your family, all of whom have had their moments of being objectionable."

"Well, you're a fine one to talk about that! Don't think

I didn't know who stole the paints out of my box to try and furbish up that ridiculous bloodstain in the library! First you took all my reds, including the vermillion, and I couldn't do any more sunsets; then you took the emerald green and the chrome yellow, which left me with nothing but indigo and Chinese white—"

"At least I didn't try to duplicate the blue blood of the Cantervilles."

"No, but what about emerald green? Who ever heard of emerald green blood?"

"Caterpillars."

"Ugh!"

"Well, what was I to do? That elder brother of yours put me in a difficult position with that cursed detergent stick of his."

"Well, I was very annoyed, but I thought you were having troubles enough as it was, so I never told on you."

"I know, and that was sporting of you. You are a dear, kind girl, Virginia—and for that reason the only person at Canterville Chase who can possibly help me."

"Really? How can I help you?"

I sank wearily into a chair with a sigh that would have done credit to Sir Henry Irving.

"I want to go to sleep and I cannot," I groaned.

Virginia's beautiful blue eyes regarded me incredulously.

"Can't sleep? Why, that's the simplest thing in the world! Even babies know how to do it."

"That may be, but I have not slept for three hundred years," I said sadly. "For three hundred years I have not slept, and I am so tired."

My words—beautifully delivered, if I do say so myself—struck home. Her lovely face grew grave, and she came over to kneel at my side, enveloping us both in a cozy cloud of steam as she looked up into my face.

"Poor, poor ghost," she murmured, "have you no place where you can sleep?"

"Far away beyond the pinewoods," I answered in a low, dreamy voice, "there is a little garden. There the grass grows long and deep, and there are the great white stars of the hemlock flowers, where the nightingale sings all night long. All night long he sings, and the cold, crystal moon looks down, and the yew tree spreads out its giant arms over the sleepers."

No romantic young girl who had been exposed to the the novelists of that day could have missed my meaning. Virginia's eyes grew dim with tears.

"You mean the Garden of Death," she whispered.

"Yes, Death. Death must be so beautiful. To lie in the soft brown earth, with the grasses waving above one's head, and listen to silence. To have no yesterday, and no to-morrow. To forget time, to forgive life, to be at peace. You can help me. You can open for me the portals of Death's house, for love is always with you, and love is stronger than Death is. With your help I may yet lie with my loved ones in yonder garden," I said, waving a dramatic hand in what I intended to be the general direction of the family burial ground. Actually I was pointing toward the vegetable garden, but then I often get mixed up when I'm inside with the drapes drawn. "Tell me, Virginia, have you ever read the old prophecy that is inscribed on my window?"

"No, how could I? I've never been here before."

"No, of course not. Silly of me to ask. I'm afraid I'm not myself today."

161

"Does the prophecy have something to do with your dying?"

"Yes."

Virginia's lips trembled.

"Then I don't want to see it—because I don't want you to go!" she declared. "We'd all miss you terribly now."

"Well, that's very flattering, Virginia, but we all have to go sometime. However, let's drop the subject—we can come back to it later. I think we've had enough of sadness for the nonce. 'Hence, loathèd Melancholy,' as Milton was wont to say in his lighter moments—which, I might add, were few and far between. Let me show you something that will bring the bloom back to your cheeks."

I had reminded myself I had better put her firmly under obligation before pressing her to do me a favour she might otherwise resist doing. Opening a cupboard, I took out the musty jewel case.

"Here is something that should solve certain problems in respect to a certain Prince Charming."

"Duke Charming," said Virginia automatically, her eyes growing round with curiosity as she gazed at the ancient case. I handed it to her.

"Just open it, if you please."

She opened it, and gasped.

"Good heavens! What are these?"

"The Henry the Eighth Rubies," I responded with a courtly bow. "The real thing. My ancestor, Good Sir Alfred, passed off a fake necklace on the king and kept the good stuff for himself. They belonged rightfully to the king the instant he demanded them, however, so no court in the land would deny that these jewels were once legally the property of a king of England. Now you can fulfil the terms of that hated clause and let those blasted guardians of Cecil's go hang!"

I chuckled.

"Of course, when it is known what these are, old Lord Grubb will have no choice but to turn them over to the authorities for inclusion in their proper place, among the Crown Jewels in the Tower, and that will really gall the old warthog, but it won't matter to you, as you will have fulfilled your obligation."

By now Virginia was starry-eyed, and so overcome that she threw her arms around me and planted a kiss on my cheek.

"Ooh, that was cold!" she said, chafing her frosted lips, "but I don't care, you're the dearest old ghost ever! How did you happen to find the jewels?"

"That secret must go with me," I replied, "to my grave. Speaking of which, my first step must be to acquaint you with the old prophecy I mentioned. If you'll kindly step over to the window . . ."

I led the way like a floorwalker and swept back the curtains. There, incised into a pane in impeccable antique lettering—"curious black letters" was Oscar's vague description—six lines of verse glinted in the sunlight:

> When a golden girl can win
> Prayer from out the lips of sin,
> When the barren almond bears,
> And a little child gives away its tears,
> Then shall all the house be still
> And peace come to Canterville.

The original concluded with "Wrackley Mill," of course; the neat substitution was mine.

"A very precious diamond inscribed those verses here long ago," I murmured.

"But I don't know what they mean," said Virginia.

"They mean," I said sadly (and here Oscar quoted me correctly), "that you must weep for me for my sins, because I have no tears, and pray with me for my soul, because I have no faith, and then, if you have always been sweet, and good, and gentle, the Angel of Death will have mercy on me. You will see fearful shapes in darkness, and wicked voices will whisper in your ear, but they will not harm you, for against the purity of a little child the powers of Hell cannot prevail."

It is almost unbelievable, the bilge one can produce when the occasion demands it. But of course, at Virginia's age, it's just the sort of stuff that goes over like a house afire. She drew herself up like Joan of Arc.

"I am not afraid," she said firmly, "and I will ask the Angel to have mercy on you."

I took her hand, the one that was not clutching the jewel case.

"Then come with me."

As I said, Oscar got that one speech down correctly, but after that he fell apart again. Our departure from the Tapestry Chamber, as he imagined it, was a perfect example of Victorian fantasizing. Oscar, you know, was completely a product of the Victorian era. It was his glory and his downfall.

As I led Virginia across the dusky room, then, he had it that "on the faded green tapestry were broidered little huntsmen. They blew their tasselled horns and their tiny hands waved her to go back. 'Go back! little Virginia,' they cried, 'go back!' but the ghost clutched her hand more tightly, and she shut her eyes against them. Horrible animals with lizard tails, and goggle eyes, blinked at her from the carven chimney-piece, and murmured, 'Beware, little Virginia, beware! We may never see you again!' but the ghost glided on more swiftly, and Virginia did not listen. When they reached the end of the room he stopped, and muttered some words she could not understand. She opened her eyes, and saw the wall slowly fading away like a mist, and a great black cavern in front of her. A bitter cold wind swept round them, and she felt something pulling at her dress. 'Quick, quick,' cried the ghost, 'or it will be too late,' and in a moment, the wainscotting had closed behind them, and the Tapestry Chamber was empty."

The *door* closed behind us, was more like it. There is no way in the world a healthy, flesh-and-blood adolescent girl like Virginia could walk through wainscotting without doing herself a great deal of damage. Oh, perhaps in some of these modern condominiums, but not in Canterville Chase.

No, we went out through the door and took my familiar route down the back staircase and then down an interminable stone spiral staircase that leaves one dizzy, and along a dank, dark passage to Robin's hideaway.

There lay Robin Clump in all his skeletal pathos. I swept a hand in his direction.

"I'm sorry to have to drag you down here, Virginia, but after all we can't have a first-class funeral without some earthly remains. Think of it! My poor bones have lain unburied these three hundred years!" I exclaimed, and pointed out some of the more touching details, such as the trencher and ewer placed just out of reach of the long fleshless fingers. Virginia was terribly shocked, of course.

"How horrible!" she cried. "You mean, her brothers really did a mean thing like this to you?"

"Yes. Family feeling ran high in those days."

She glanced at the skeleton and then at me.

"You look shorter there than you do now."

"Skeletons shrink—and of course, ghosts tend to be tall."

"Oh."

She sniffed, and I assumed she was about to weep, but instead she said, "It smells like someone's been smoking in here!"

I protested rather loudly.

"That's hardly possible. These old dungeons always have a peculiar odour."

"Are you sure Wash hasn't been sneaking down here? I know he's bought a pipe."

"Wash? Certainly not!"

"Oh. Well . . ."

For a moment she stood gazing down piteously at the pathetic relics, and the atmosphere of the place began to get to her. Her tears began to flow and, kneeling beside the skeleton and setting the jewel case aside, she clasped her hands and began to pray silently. When she had finished, she rose and faced me with a quiet dignity beyond her tender years.

"I shall inform Lord Canterville and my family, and your poor dear remains shall be given the proper burial you have yearned for so long in vain. We shall give you an absolutely *dreamy* funeral!"

"Dreamy? Where did you get that word?"

"I don't know. It just popped out."

I was not only impressed, I was awed.

"Virginia, this day you have bridged the centuries, you have spoken in the tongue of another age. Time means nothing here," I told her, and bowed over her hand. "Thank you, my dear. Thank you."

166

Fortunately I did not have to conceal my happiness, though it emanated from a source other than what she supposed. I was recalling the terms Lady Eleanore had conveyed to me:

"Before you will ever be permitted to leave Canterville Chase, you must first be *officially* declared dead and buried."

Silently I led my young helper away, up, up, up to the lower landing of the back staircase. And there I took my leave.

"You have freed me," I told her. Virginia stood clutching the jewel case to her young bosom. She had never looked more appealing. Her eyes misted over, and of all her tears, those were the ones I cherished.

"We'll miss you, Sir Simon," she said once more. "We'll miss you dreadfully."

I bowed my head.

"Thank you again, my dear—and farewell!"

Stepping back, and throwing her a heartfelt kiss as I touched my fingers to my lips, I turned toward the wainscotting and disappeared from her sight forever.

eighteen

ALL THIS TOOK a while, of course, and afterwards I had to report to Lady Eleanore. By the time she left, it was well into the breakfast hour, which normally would have found me in the library waiting to see how things were going with Wash and Sheila. I hurried over, but with no hope of being more than an observer of the passing show. Regretfully I faced the fact that there was simply not time enough left for me to do anything to assist young love in that quarter. I had Mr. Holmes to think about. Even now he and Dr. Watson were bearing down on us aboard the train from London. It seemed only prudent to be safely out of the way before he appeared and began putting two and two together in his inimitable fashion. Lady Eleanore, seeing the funeral as a fait accompli, was confident she could get clearance for me on this score.

"I don't doubt They will agree. I am sure They will not want to take chances; I am sure They would not put it past Mr. Holmes to lay even the Canterville Ghost by the heels and deliver him into custody," she declared.

Even so, there was still time for one last visit to the library. When I arrived, lovely Sheila, faithful as always to the furniture, was working away, her auburn hair glorious in the morning light that streamed through the stained-glass window. And I had hardly settled myself on my accustomed perch when Wash came striding in.

According to Lady Eleanore, on top of everything else he had been enflaming himself with the poetry of Algernon Charles Swinburne, who was considered pretty hot stuff in those days. Given Wash's condition, this was certainly carrying coals to Newcastle, but in any event it did nothing to reduce his head of steam. As he entered the room, it was plain that the mere sight of Sheila was enough to make him start giving off heat waves.

"Darling!"

Wild-eyed and determined, he bore down on her. She dropped her polishing cloth and backed away.

"Oh, sir, spare me!" she begged piteously.

He seized her hand.

"Please! Listen to me! I have no wicked designs on you, Sheila, I am here to— Well, I've made up my mind, and— Dearest Sheila, will you marry me?"

"*Washington!*"

The response came not from Sheila but from the pop-eyed turkey-cock in the doorway. Needless to say, his paternal roar froze the hapless pair into a tableau that could have gone straight into Madame Tussaud's Wax Museum. The Minister turned to loose another roar in the direction of the breakfast room.

"Lucretia! Come in here!"

Mrs. Otis appeared at something more than her usual stately pace.

"Hiram, whatever is the matter?"

"*Everything* is the matter! This son of yours—"

How the Minister might have described the situation was lost to posterity, for at that instant the sounds of a carriage

169

approaching the front of the house could be heard via the great entrance hall, where the front door had been opened to admit the warming rays of the sun.

"Oh, good Lord, someone's coming!" groaned the Minister. "It must be Mr. Holmes and Dr. Watson! They must have caught an earlier train! Now, I'll go greet them, and the rest of you stay here and *act natural!*" he ordered, and bustled away leaving them looking about as natural as one of those tableaux I mentioned.

No one was more anxious to find out if the minister's assumptions were correct than I was. Little did he know that I reached the hall as quickly as he did—and both of us made it well ahead of Shadwell, the butler.

To my vast relief it was not Sherlock Holmes who stepped down from the carriage. Rather it was a portly, authoritative-looking gentleman, who might have been a larger British version of the American Minister himself. Hurrying out, the Minister walked to the top of the broad steps to meet him.

"Minister Otis, I presume?"

"Yes, sir?"

"I am Sir Lansing Carruthers," said the stranger, offering his hand. "Mr. Sherlock Holmes has asked me to be present at Canterville Chase this morning, having assured me that matters requiring my special knowledge may transpire."

"Sir Lansing Carruthers?" cried the Minister. "Well, I'll be blowed! You are the famous gemologist, I believe, the one who—"

"Spare my blushes, sir," said Sir Lansing, bowing with patently false modesty as he unblushingly stole a line from Holmes' own repertoire.

"Well—er—well, come in and make yourself at home, Sir

Lansing!" urged the Minister, recovering himself. "We're expecting Mr. Holmes on the 10:40 train, so he should be here by eleven thirty at the latest. . . ."

Whilst they came inside, I hurried back to my perch. I was there in time to see them enter.

"Lucretia, look who's here!" said Minister Otis, bowing Sir Lansing through the door. "It's Sir Lansing Carruthers—"

"*Sheila!*"

Sir Lansing had stopped in his tracks and was staring at our parlourmaid with popping eyes in a rapidly reddening face.

"Sheila, what are you doing here—and in that ridiculous getup? You're supposed to be in Rome, studying art! Is this another of your blasted social experiments?"

"Daddy!" Sheila should have swooned into Wash's arms, but she was not the swooning type. "What are *you* doing here, of all places?"

"Dash it all, girl, why shouldn't I be here? Mr. Sherlock Holmes—"

"Oh, for heaven's sake! It's those silly jewels!"

Sir Lansing's face tended dangerously toward the purple end of the spectrum.

"Silly . . . jewels? You call . . . jewels . . . *silly?*"

"Oh, Daddy, you know I don't mean that. It's just that —well, of all times, just when—"

It is wonderful to see what one-track minds people have, the way they can always keep their own interest firmly in view no matter what may be going on around them. At any rate, Master Washington chose this very moment to step forward with a pale face and blurt out,

"Sir, I want to marry your daughter!"

That almost did it for Sir Lansing. He stood transfixed, gasping like a fish out of water. Which gave Wash time to turn to Sheila and say,

"Sheila, *will* you marry me?"

Sheila's pretty face was a study in harebrained contrasts.

"Oh, Wash, I don't know!" she babbled. "When I was supposed to be unworthy of you, I felt worthy of you; but now that I'm worthy of you, I feel unworthy of you!"

Wash stared at her for a throbbing moment, and then he seemed to change before our very eyes. Suddenly he somehow expanded and grew into those puppy paws and feet of his. Suddenly Wash the boy was gone, and Washington the man had taken his place. Reaching out in a masterly way, Washington took one of Sheila's wrists in a firm grasp.

"Sheila, come outside," he ordered. "I want to talk to you—alone."

And while the rest of us watched silently, he dragged her toward the door, past her father, past his, out into the great entrance hall and through the open door. Her feeble protests died away into the shrubbery. Sir Lansing watched this performance with an expression that went from outrage to stupefaction to dawning satisfaction.

"Bless my soul!" he growled. "If there's anything that girl needs . . ."

He turned with a tooth-grinding smile to his host.

"Minister Otis, do you happen to have a spot of whisky in the house?"

"I certainly do, sir," said the Minister, "and the sooner we locate it, the better! This way!"

nineteen

THE MORNING was well advanced when I met Lady Eleanore for our final tryst in the dense shrubbery near the family burial ground. She looked me up and down with admiring eyes.

"Well, Simon, I must say those clothes become you."

For my departure I had selected a conservatively tailored dark suit of contemporary design such as any well-bred Englishman of that day might have worn when travelling, so that if anyone happened to glimpse me along the way, I would not look out of place.

"Well, I must say your frock becomes you, too, Elly," I responded. "I am thankful my last sight of you does not have to be as Mrs. Umney."

"So am I."

I began to feel ill at ease, the way one does during the final moments on a train platform.

"Well, Elly, I'll miss you. It's been a real pleasure lately, especially last night. Like old times. I mean, like when we were first . . ."

"It was lovely. Speaking of which," she murmured, and brought forth from its snug nest in the bosom of her frock a small black book. She looked at me with steadfast eyes.

"I'm sure you won't want your special dispensation to go to waste, so this will help you keep out of trouble. Our Witches' Code forbids us to be jealous or possessive. Share and share alike is our watchword. So I have prepared a list of names and addresses of some of my more attractive sisters for you, and I'm sure they'll make you welcome."

Now, here was a prize any ghost fortunate enough to be in my position should have been willing to give his all for, and I knew it, and yet I had to force a lecherous smile onto my face as I accepted it. What was the matter with me?

"Elly, thank you!" I said, ogling it with hollow enthusiasm. "I'll give each and every one of them your regards, and try to make you proud of me in every case."

"I'm sure you will, Simon. Tell me, where do you plan to go first?"

"Oh, I don't know. Anywhere but France. I thought perhaps I'd do a bit of Italy again, for a starter—perhaps spend a day or two in Venice. . . ."

With a self-conscious smile, I issued an invitation I strove to keep light and playful.

"Elly, why don't you take a vacation and come along? We'd have a great time."

"I wish I could, but I can't."

"Oh. Have to stay here?"

"Yes."

"Well, but for how long?"

"For . . . indefinitely."

"Oh. Well, I'm sorry. I'll miss you. I really will."

"And I will miss you, Simon."

Her simple reply sent such a sharp twinge of pain through me that I quickly changed the subject.

"Are all the young lovers happy now?"

She laughed.

"Oh, yes. Wash and Sheila are floating around together, trailing clouds of bliss. The only condition she finally insisted on is that she will remain in service here until she's finished the library furniture—she's the kind who can't abide not to finish a job once she's started it. Her father says she's always been that way. As for Virginia and Cecil, they've gathered the family together, including Lord Canterville, and are at this very moment revealing their great secret."

I clapped a hand to my forehead.

"Oh, damn! I *knew* I'd forget something! I forgot to return Cecil's ring!"

"Never mind—I fetched it from your room and took care of it."

"Elly, you're wonderful!"

"When Cecil finally left his room this morning, I was on the watch for him. He was looking more pale and drawn than even Dr. Dobell could account for, so I knew at once what was troubling him. I curtseyed and held out the ring. 'This was found in the shrubbery, my lord,' I said. 'I think you must have dropped it there.' Of course he was overjoyed, and at the same time turned quite red in the face. 'Oh, how can I thank you, Mrs. Umney!' he said. 'I—er—I borrowed it from an old aunt of mine, and I should have hated to—er—misplace it.'"

I chuckled heartily.

"Young jackanapes! I wondered how he had managed a stone of those dimensions. Well, it certainly stood us all in good stead, and I'm only sorry they can't know how really precious it is to them."

"So am I. I'm really quite pleased with Cecil. He also thanked me very nicely for the chicken soup I sent up to him."

From the house the mellow-throated clock announced the half hour. Half-past eleven. Distinguished visitors were due at any moment now. It was time for me to leave. I glanced at Lady Eleanore, and looked away again. It was all very well to change subjects and talk about other things, but I could not escape the thoughts that were really occupying the forefront of my mind with steadily increasing cruelty. So now I cleared my throat and reverted to them.

"Listen, though, Elly, there must be *some* way you can get away from this blasted place now and then, so that we can have a little get-together from time to time."

Dropping her lovely eyes, she shook her head.

"No, Simon, I cannot."

"Then we will never see each other again?"

"I'm afraid not," she said, and I could have sworn there was a catch in her voice, even something close to a sob. At the sound of it, everything became clear to me—about myself, that is—and I burst out in the wildest manner but with complete conviction.

"Well, if that's how it is, then I won't go!"

Her head came up quickly at that.

"What?"

"I won't go! I'll stay right here with you at Canterville Chase, and that's that!"

"Simon! In spite of the Minister, and Washington, and the twins, and now Mr. Holmes, who may well put you in jeopardy?"

"Yes! In spite of everything! Don't you see, Elly, I can't leave you! I . . . dammit, woman, I love you!"

Tears welled up in her eyes, but not even tears could dim them at that moment. She was suddenly radiant.

"And I love you, too! Oh, Simon, you have done the one thing that could set me free to be with you!"

I stared at her, hardly daring to hope I had heard aright.

"What? A little thing like that? Three little words, as they say?"

"Three little words are nothing unless they are true, Simon, but it's plain you really mean them."

"I do, I do! And you really mean that you can— Oh, Elly!" I clasped her to me. "Go get your things! We haven't a moment to lose!"

Rosy-cheeked and beaming, she pushed me away.

"I can't go this minute, silly! I have to round things off here in a proper manner as Mrs. Umney. I'll have to give a month's notice—but after that . . ."

"A month! Well . . . that's not too bad—"

"Not half so bad as an eternity."

"There's something in that! In fact, actually it might all work out very well. I'll go on ahead and find a nice palazzo for us to stay in, and—"

I broke off to regard her with a fond twinkle in my eye, and took out the little black book.

"And by the way," I said, "I won't be needing this."

Lady Eleanore blushed.

"Our Code forbids possessiveness," she reminded me, "— but I was *hoping* you'd give it back."

At that moment the clatter of a dogcart interrupted our raptures. The shrubbery prevented us from seeing it, but we could hear every word spoken by its occupants.

"Stop here, driver!" cried a sharp, commanding voice. "Here we are, Watson, and yonder stands the great family crypt of the Cantervilles. Notice the two sets of footprints approaching and leaving the door of the crypt, one set those of a man, the other those of a woman."

"Good Lord, Holmes," cried another voice, "can you see them from *here*?"

"To the trained eye, Watson, such trifles are obvious. Less obvious, perhaps, are the curious imprints of two other smaller pairs of barefooted prints which I now see may be added to our clues. I have no doubt that careful measurements of all these will afford us valuable information. Let us alight and have a look in there before continuing on to the house."

We heard their eager footsteps approach the crypt, heard the door being tugged open, heard them go inside.

"I am sorry to miss any of this," I whispered to Lady Eleanore. "In fact, I hate to miss my own funeral. I console myself with the thought that poor Robin Clump will finally have a decent grave to lie in—and among his betters, at that. However, I must be off. Be sure to get word to me as to when you're coming, so that I can meet you with a gondola."

From inside the crypt came a series of "Ah-ha's!" and "Observe these marks, Watson!" A moment later the two came outside.

"The jewels were there, Watson—mark my words, they were there, and have only quite recently been extracted. Excellent, excellent! This case promises to be not without its interesting aspects. I shall be most eager to hear further particulars from Lord Canterville himself—and here, if I am not mistaken, is our distinguished client now, and with him Sir Lansing Carruthers!"

"Mr. Holmes! Mr. Holmes!" Now we could hear the voice of my lineal descendant, who seemed to be hurrying toward them. "The ruby necklace has been found, and the earthly remains of the Canterville Ghost as well!"

"I have already deduced where the jewels were discovered," retorted the great detective. "Would you be good enough to lead me to the dungeon where the bones were discovered?"

"My word!" cried Lord Canterville. "Mr. Holmes, how did you know the bones were found in a dungeon?"

"I shall be glad to explain that," said Holmes, "when we are on the scene."

The men walked toward the house. I turned to Lady Eleanore and held out my arms.

"Now I really must go. But it will be a long month! I can't wait till we're together again! We'll have a second honeymoon!"

"We certainly will. But you're quite right, Simon, we must stop dawdling here in the shrubbery like—well, like the children. I must change into my Umneys and return to my duties in the house before my absence causes comment."

"Very well, then—*arrivederci*, my love!"

"*Arrivederci*, my sweet!"

Thinning myself out, I turned and sped away round the rear of the family burial ground, across the park, and down toward the lake. There I paused and turned back for a final look at the place that had been my home for more than three hundred years.

The great house basked in the sunshine. Lord Canterville, Sir Lansing, Holmes, and Dr. Watson were ascending the broad front steps that led to the main entrance, where the American Minister was waiting. Mrs. Umney was stumping across the lawn with a businesslike stride that boded ill for malingering housemaids. One of those maids was behind a huge oak being kissed by Wash. She was standing tiptoe on one dainty foot with her other leg bent up behind her. Virginia and Cecil were trailing along behind the distinguished visitors, no doubt eager to see as much as they could of the famous detective in action. The morning sun flashed fire from a large, brilliant object on Miss Virginia's left hand.

Just as the men reached the entrance, Mr. Holmes clapped his hand to his neck and cried, "Ouch!" My glance shifted just quickly enough to observe two pea-shooters being withdrawn from sight in the large oriel window. I released a shout of laughter and flung up my hand in a warning.

"Beware, Mr. Holmes, beware! I speak from experience —beware! You may have met your match at last!"

With a light heart I turned away and set my course for Venice.